"What do we do?" she whispered, her lips moving against his finger.

"This," he said, and he whirled her around and pressed her back against the brick wall of the stairwell. She gasped just as he lowered his mouth to hers.

Not only did he cover her mouth with his but also he covered her body, too. To hide her. To protect her.

That had been his intent. But her lips were soft beneath his, her breath warm, and he found himself really kissing her. He moved his mouth over hers, taking advantage of her parted lips to deepen the kiss.

And her arms moved between them. Instead of pushing him away, as he expected, they linked around his neck. And she clung to him.

AGENT UNDERCOVER

Lisa Childs

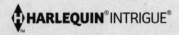

With love and appreciation for my dad—Jack Childs.
You will always be my hero!

ISBN-13: 978-0-373-69828-8

Agent Undercover

Copyright © 2015 by Lisa Childs

Recycling programs
for this product may
not exist in your area.

Printed in U.S.A.

Lisa Childs writes paranormal and contemporary romance for Harlequin. She lives on thirty acres in Michigan with her two daughters, a talkative Siamese and a long-haired Chihuahua who thinks she's a rottweiler. Lisa loves hearing from readers, who can contact her through her website, lisachilds.com, or snail-mail address, PO Box 139, Marne, MI 49435.

Books by Lisa Childs

HARLEQUIN INTRIGUE

Visit the Author Profile page at
Harlequin.com for more titles

CAST OF CHARACTERS

Special Agent Ash Stryker—The FBI agent has a lot of experience going undercover for dangerous assignments with the Anti-Terrorism Division, but his most dangerous assignment will be going undercover with Claire Molenski.

Claire Molenski—The former hacker now ensures that others can't hack into government and other important security sites, but she finds herself under suspicion and undercover with an FBI agent who's as handsome as he is aggravating.

Peter Nowak—The former CIA agent had started a consulting company to ensure that government and other companies couldn't be hacked, but maybe security hadn't been his agenda...

Martin Crouch—Claire's assistant doesn't have her skills or her integrity.

Leslie Morrison—Claire's former mentor had retired—or had he?

Agent Sally Burnham—The young agent was supposed to be helping protect Claire, but she might prove a greater danger.

Special Agent Dalton Reyes—The agent grew up on the streets of Chicago, so he has torn allegiances between the law and the people with whom he grew up. Should Ash have trusted him?

Chapter One

Special Agent Ashton Stryker's heart pounded fast and hard with anticipation and a rush of adrenaline. He was about to meet the greatest threat to national security in his career with the FBI's antiterrorism division. Ash's responsibility was to neutralize that threat.

A bell chimed, announcing his time up with the woman across the table from him. She may have said hi. He wasn't certain; he hadn't been paying any attention to her. His target was farther down the long table, smiling at the man whose hand she shook before he moved on to the woman to her left.

Had she passed anything to him in that handshake? Ash wasn't close enough to see, but there were other eyes on her. Other agents had her under surveillance, too.

Ash stood up and took the next chair down the table. He was getting closer to her. The bell chimed again, announcing the beginning of the next five minutes.

"How can you look like that and be so socially awkward?" the woman across from him asked.

His focus on his target, he only spared the woman a glance. She was probably old enough to be his mother—maybe his grandmother—with iron-gray hair and small reading glasses hanging from a chunky gold chain around the neck of the sweatshirt embroidered with cats. "Excuse me?"

"You haven't said anything to the women before me," she said. "Of course when you look like that—the epitome of tall, dark and handsome—you probably don't have to say anything. You could grunt and women would go home with you."

He felt like grunting with frustration and impatience, but then she might take that as an invitation. "I'm sorry," he said. "This is the first time I've come to one of these things—"

"It's called speed dating," she said. "You only have five minutes, so you have to talk fast."

"I would rather listen," he said. It was what he did. Listening was how he had found the threat. He'd picked up chatter on wiretaps and other surveillance and then he'd found the post himself.

"Oh—" the older woman fanned herself with one of the drink menus "—you look like that and you'd rather listen. No wonder you've never come to one of these things before. You haven't had to. Why are you here tonight?"

Obviously he couldn't answer honestly. Ash was no rookie when it came to going undercover; he'd had some dangerous assignments over the years, going deep undercover in terrorist camps and militia groups as well as a motorcycle gang.

But he had never gone speed dating before. A couple of chairs earlier, someone had run a stiletto heel up his pant leg. Another woman had tried to give him her room key. There was danger here, too. So Ash had to be careful to not blow his cover.

"Why?" the woman asked again, her voice sharp with impatience that he hadn't answered yet.

She definitely reminded him of his grandmother, at least as much as he could remember of the austere woman from whom his father had run away as a teenager. After he'd gotten married and had Ash, he'd come back to visit, but Grandma hadn't approved of Ash's mother any more than she had her own son.

Because the woman was kind of intimidating and because it was easier to sell a cover if you told as much of the truth as possible, Ash replied honestly, "I want to meet someone."

The woman emitted a wistful sigh. "You will," she assured him. "You will."

He glanced down the table again to where the threat chatted easily with the man across from her. He was bald with no neck and an ill-fitting suit. Was he a buyer?

"Ooooh," the woman across from Ash said as if she'd just learned something momentous.

Had he given himself away?

He turned back to her and found her studying him through the thick lenses of her small glasses.

"You already have your eye on someone," she said, and she pointed down the table at the threat.

Ash swallowed a groan. He had given himself away. So he offered the woman a sheepish grin. "Am I that obvious?"

She shrugged. "I'm observant. I don't think she's noticed you at all, though. And in my opinion, you could do better than that pale little blonde."

It could have been the crimson shade of her tight dress or the pale yellow of her hair that made her skin look translucent. But he knew it wasn't—even while he admired the fit of that dress and the bright shade of lipstick on her wide mouth and the shimmer of her light hair.

The woman snorted derisively. "She looks like she hasn't been out in the daylight for years."

Ash knew why Claire Molenski looked that way. She *hadn't* been out in the daylight for years. And if he had his way, he would be locking her back up again soon.

He just had to catch her before she and her greed put into motion an economic and security catastrophe of epic proportions.

CLAIRE'S HEAD WAS THROBBING, and the smile felt frozen on her face. Her lips were so dry that they were now stuck to her teeth, so she couldn't pull them down again. *This is what you wanted*, she reminded herself.

A new life. A life that wasn't so lonely and empty.

She doubted she was going to find that new life in the dining room of the Waterview Inn, though. Most of the guys were much older than she was and some, from the deep indents on their ring fingers, were not as eligible as they claimed. In fact, when she sneezed, one pulled out a handkerchief for her and whipped out his ring as well, which rolled across the grape-leaf-and-vine-patterned carpet.

She giggled as he chased after it. But then that strange feeling assailed her—as if everyone was staring at her. She looked around the room but noticed no one overtly studying her. Maybe she was just paranoid because she hadn't been out in public for a while—for a long while.

That was the whole purpose of coming here. She could have just signed up for online dating. But she'd wanted to go out and actually meet real people—people with personality and character. Only she hadn't yet met anyone she cared to date. The bell dinged again, so she drew in a deep breath to brace herself for the next man to take the chair across from her.

First she looked at his hands, which he'd braced on the table in front of him. The ring finger held no telltale indentation. So she glanced up, and the breath she'd drawn escaped in a gasp of surprise.

Very pleasant surprise. This man wasn't too old for her. His hair was thick and black, and his eyes were a piercing blue. So piercing that he seemed to peer right through her. Had it been his stare that she'd felt earlier?

"Hello," she said. "My name's Claire."

So many of the other men had remarked that it was odd that such a young woman had such an old-fashioned name, but he just nodded, almost as if he'd known her name. But she had never met him before; he was the kind of man a woman would never forget meeting.

So she was definitely just paranoid.

"What's your name?" she asked when he didn't freely offer it.

"Ash," he replied almost reluctantly.

She floundered around for something clever to say, but her mind was blank. Maybe it was because he was so damn good-looking; maybe it was just because she had no idea how to date anymore. It had been too long.

She had read some books about how to flirt when dating. But none of what she read came to her mind. It remained blank, which was a novelty since she was usually unable to stop thinking.

"What do you do for a living, Claire?" he asked.

Several other men had asked that same question, but she actually wanted to tell him the truth. "I work with computers," she said.

"A programmer?"

She was more like a deprogrammer, but she didn't want to explain that. Legally, she really couldn't. So she just nodded. "Yes, it's boring. What about you?" she asked. "What do you do for a living?"

"Government job," he replied. "It's boring, too."

"Politics?" she asked. With that face, she could see him smiling at voters, kissing babies, shaking hands...

He shook his head. "That probably wouldn't be boring."

"Probably not," she agreed. "So you have a desk job, too?"

"Sometimes," he replied.

He had that whole mysterious thing going on, which had probably worked well for him with some of the other women. But Claire wasn't looking for complicated. She'd already had enough of that in her life. She was looking for simple and open and honest and fun—which was why none of the other men had worked for her, either.

Finally the smile left her face. She didn't have the strength to make the effort to fake it anymore. "I'm sorry," she said. "I shouldn't be here."

Maybe she wasn't ready. Maybe she hadn't done enough research. Maybe it was that feeling of being watched—even if she was totally wrong—that unnerved her.

"Aren't you available after all?" he asked.

Again she felt as if he asked a question to which he already knew the answer. She shook her head and tried to shake off her uncharacteristic paranoia. "That's not it," she said. "I'm just not ready..."

She pushed back her chair and stood up as he stood up, too. He towered over her in height and breadth with his impossibly wide shoulders and chest. His black sweater and dress pants made him look incredibly handsome and incredibly imposing. She definitely wasn't ready—especially not for him.

She couldn't believe someone like him would have even come to a speed dating event. He had to have women throwing themselves at him constantly. He didn't belong here, either. But she would leave it up to him to figure that out.

"I have to go," she said, and now panic was joining the paranoia, pressing down on her chest so that she struggled to draw a breath.

"Are you okay?" he asked.

"I need some air…" She whirled around so quickly that she knocked over her chair before rushing from the room.

His deep voice called after her, "I hope it wasn't something I said…"

A woman Claire passed on her way out laughed. "That's not likely…"

Claire heard nothing else but the sound of her own pulse pounding in her ears. What about that man had made her so nervous?

She hadn't even waited for the bell to ding before leaving him. For some reason she hadn't dared. Maybe it was the feeling he already knew things about her that she hadn't told him that had unnerved her. Or had it been the way he had looked at her—as if he could see right through her?

Or maybe it had just been the way he looked—too handsome. Dating him would be like going from a bicycle to racing motorcycles. If she was going to start dating, she needed to start on the bicycle with training wheels.

She had taken a room in the hotel for the night in case she'd had too much to drink and hadn't wanted to risk her life or anyone else's by driving. But she had barely taken more than a sip of her glass of wine, so she could drive herself home. She would feel safer in her apartment than this hotel. As she crossed the lobby, she felt as if even the eyes in the portraits were following her. She didn't need to go up to the room since all her overnight things were still in her oversize purse. So she headed straight for the front doors.

Night had fallen since the speed dating event had started. Even with the streetlights, the parking lot was dark. This hotel was outside the city of Chicago, so it had no parking garage and no valet service. She had to find her own vehicle but at least the lot was just out in front of the hotel.

She was reaching inside her bag, digging for her keys, when someone grabbed her. A strong arm wrapped tightly around her, binding her arms to her sides, as the man lifted her off her feet. She parted her lips to scream, but a big hand clamped down hard over her mouth, muffling her cry for help and nearly smothering her.

Or maybe it wasn't the hand but the handkerchief it held against her mouth and nose that smothered her—with the sweet, cloying scent of chloroform.

If she didn't fight fast and hard, she would soon lose her chance.

And maybe her life...

Chapter Two

"I lost eyes on her." A voice emanated from Ash's earpiece. It was a two-way radio that transmitted what he said and what the other agents said. "She's gone…"

Claire Molenski had stepped through the front doors of the hotel and disappeared into the darkness. Ash had followed her from the dining room, but at a discreet distance that had only drawn the attention of the older woman who had earlier noticed him staring at Claire. The woman had winked at him, either teasing him or encouraging him. Ash had waited only a few minutes before exiting those lobby doors and stepping into the lot.

"Where the hell has she gone?" he asked the question more to himself than to the other agents who could hear him through their earpieces. He hadn't been far behind her.

"We lost the visual on the subject," another agent remarked.

Ash cursed. How had she slipped the surveillance so easily? The woman was a bigger threat than even he had realized. And from the minute her name had come to his attention, she'd had his full attention. He'd known this woman was going to be dangerous.

He stepped deeper into the shadows of the dimly lit parking lot. And he heard something. Something muffled and soft—like a crying kitten—was just loud enough to draw his attention. There were plenty of strays in the questionable outskirts of Chicago.

But was it a trick? A lure?

He moved carefully between the parked cars, keeping low so that no one noticed him. But he noticed a dark shadow, probably of a man, bent over as he lifted something from the asphalt. Lights flashed on as a car started, dispelling the shadow to the image of a hulky bald-headed man. The light shimmered off the pale blond hair of the woman that the man carried.

Claire.

Her head lolled back, her eyes closed. She was either unconscious or dead. That cry Ash had heard must have been her last weak attempt to scream for help. Had he heard her too late? But if she was dead, why was the man carrying her? To dispose of the body?

Ash reached beneath his sweater and drew his gun from his holster. He could have spoken into the radio and signaled for help. But then he might have also made the man aware of his presence. And if he was going to overpower him, he needed the element of surprise.

So he crept through the rows of parked cars as the driver of the vehicle with the lights honked and rolled down his window. Ash had thought it was an accomplice. But the driver called out, "Is everything okay? Is she okay?"

"Just had too much to drink," the man murmured, his accent so thick the words were hard to comprehend.

The driver hesitated yet, his car idling in the lot. He must have realized what Ash had—that the situation wasn't right. At the very least it wasn't what the man claimed. Ash had only seen Claire take one sip of her wine and no more. Had it been drugged?

Maybe that was why she had rushed off the way she had. But she had been clear-eyed and coherent then. Whatever had happened to her had happened after she'd stepped through the doors of the hotel and out of Ash's sight. It had happened so damn quickly that he'd nearly lost her—and still might.

"Why don't we call hotel security?" the driver suggested.

The man slung Claire over one arm and pulled a gun with his other. He pointed the barrel through the open window of the car. "Why don't you mind your own damn business?"

Chivalry forgotten now, the driver sped off—tires squealing as the car careened out of the lot. The car had drawn the attention of other agents, who ran across the lot toward the man.

Ash stepped from the shadows, the barrel of his gun pointing at the man's heart. Claire was slung over his other shoulder, and so small that Ash wouldn't hit her if he fired. Or at least he hoped he wouldn't...

"She is my business," Ash said. "So you can put her down now or you can take a bullet."

The big man scoffed. "You will shoot me?"

Ash shrugged. "Either I will shoot you or one of the other FBI agents will."

All around them, guns cocked. Ash hoped all of those guns belonged to fellow agents. But some could have belonged to this man's associates. Would he have attempted this abduction alone? Which country or group might they be from?

"Put her down," Ash said.

"I could kill her," the man threatened.

"If that was the plan," Ash said, "she would already be dead. But then she wouldn't be worth anything."

The threat she posed would have been eliminated, though. Ash's assignment accomplished. But that gave him no sense of relief—only regret. Anger surged through him, heating his blood despite the cool night air. He had no intention of letting this man, or anyone else, kill Claire Molenski.

The man turned his weapon on Ash, pointing the barrel at him. "Then I will kill you—"

Before he could fire, someone else took the shot, and the big man crumpled to the asphalt. Ash lunged forward and caught Claire before she could hit the ground, too. She was incredibly light and small, more like the weight and size of a child than a woman. But there was nothing innocent or vulnerable about her. He had to remind himself of that; he had to remind himself that she was the danger.

But because of what she knew—and how many nefarious groups and governments wanted that knowledge—she was also in danger. Some people or countries weren't able or willing to pay for the information she had; instead they would torture her for it.

Ash had seen men three times her size break. Claire Molenski wouldn't survive. So just watching her wasn't going to be enough to keep her safe. But protecting her, like she needed protection, would make it harder to gather enough evidence for her arrest.

HER HEART POUNDING WILDLY, Claire awoke in a panic. She had no idea how long she had been unconscious, if it had been minutes or hours since she'd been chloroformed.

Where had she been taken? She blinked her eyes wide, trying to clear her fuzzy vision and her fuzzy head. But the room was dark.

She reached out and breathed a sigh of relief that

her hands weren't bound. Her fingers skimmed across silky material, and she recognized the soft surface on which she was lying. She had been carried to a bed. She skimmed her hands down her body and breathed another sigh of relief that she still wore her dress. Maybe nobody had hurt her.

Yet.

But then a lamp snapped on, and she blinked against the brightness of the light shining in her eyes. "What— where am I?"

"Your room," a deep voice replied.

She couldn't see him—not with the light filling her vision field with spots. Who was he?

And why was he lying to her?

This wasn't her room. Her bed wasn't this soft and smooth. Her mattress was old and lumpy, but since she was rarely home, she hadn't seen the reason to replace it. Or to make the bed, either. Her sheets were never smooth. They were always rumpled, usually kicked to a tangled mess at the foot of the bed, as she rushed to get to the office. She was pretty much always at work—before the sun rose in the morning until after it set again at night.

"Why did you grab me?" she asked, her pulse still racing. While she wasn't bound, she *had* been abducted.

He replied matter-of-factly, "So you wouldn't hit the ground."

"I wasn't going to fall…" She blinked again, and her eyes adjusted to the light enough that she could make him out standing over the bed.

He was tall—taller than she had even realized when she'd talked to him across the table earlier. And he was so broad. No wonder he had overpowered her so easily in the parking lot in the dark. If only she'd seen him coming, maybe she could have outrun him.

Then she remembered the heels she'd been wearing; he would have caught her and easily once she had twisted her ankle. She wiggled her toes, grateful that her shoes were gone. Maybe she could run now.

"Why?" she asked, her fears growing even more. "Why would you bring me here?"

"This is your room," he repeated. "The one you rented at the hotel."

"Oh…" She had rented a room. But she had changed her mind about using it. Obviously he'd had other plans.

"Why did you drug me?" she asked, although she was afraid that she knew the answer.

Was he the kind of man who didn't take rejection well? With the way he looked, he probably wasn't often rejected. Did he intend to take what she hadn't been willing to offer him?

"I didn't drug you," he said.

"Someone grabbed me in the parking lot," she said, "and put something over my mouth and nose…"

"Chloroform," he replied again so matter-of-factly.

"So you admit to using it on me?" she asked, and anger joined her fear. And again she was grateful her hands weren't bound because she would fight him. She would hurt him as badly as he intended to hurt her.

"No," he said. "I recognized the smell. That's why I brought you back to your room, so you could regain consciousness."

"What do you intend to do to me?" she asked, her heart continuing to pound wildly with fear.

He sighed and pushed a hand through his dark hair. "I wish I knew…"

"Then why did you grab me?" If he had no plan…

"I only grabbed you after your abductor had been shot," he said, as if his crazy explanation made perfect sense.

"Abductor?" So now he was trying to place the blame on someone else.

He nodded. "I don't know who the man was."

"Was?"

He nodded again but grimly this time, his strong-looking jaw clenched. "He's gone."

"Dead?" Her voice squeaked with the question. "You killed him?" Maybe there had really been another man… before he'd died.

"No," he said. "Another agent shot him…before he could shoot me."

"And then you brought me back here," she said, as if she was following his preposterous story. The man was obviously deranged. No wonder he'd followed her out of the hotel and tried to grab her.

And she had thought getting to know someone in person first would be safer than dating someone she'd only met online. Maybe dating at all was a bad idea. But how else was she ever going to meet someone who could share her life—her hopes, her dreams?

Somehow she suspected that having a relationship wasn't going to be an issue for her anymore—unless she could somehow overpower this muscular man and escape him. She tried to peer around him to determine how far away the door was.

Or maybe she could yell…

Weren't hotel room walls notoriously thin?

She opened her mouth to scream, but his palm slid across her lips, silencing her. And he joined her on the bed, his thigh hard and warm against her hip. She tried to struggle, but he easily held her down—pushing her into the mattress. And she noticed that his sweater had ridden up, revealing a holster and a gun. He was armed.

Tears stung her eyes as fear overwhelmed her. What was he going to do to her?

"I'm not going to hurt you," he said, almost as if he regretted that he wasn't. "I've been watching you…"

So she hadn't been paranoid.

"I'm trying to stop you from doing something that's going to put your life and the country in danger," he said. "But obviously I'm too late. You're already in danger."

She had realized that back in the parking lot. She'd been scared then. She was terrified now.

"Have you put the country in danger, too?" he asked.

She moved her lips against his palm, as if she was trying to answer his question. As if she could actually answer something so absurd…

She only wanted him to move his hand so that she could scream. If he didn't want her making any noise, he wouldn't risk shooting her. Would he?

If she screamed, hopefully someone would hear her and come to her aid. It was her only chance to escape this man and his madness.

But he didn't move his hand. In fact, it covered her entire face, his fingers covering one ear and his thumb the other. She could still hear him, though—still hear his ridiculous questions.

"Did you already endanger national security?" he asked.

"How?" she murmured the word against his palm.

Who did he think she was? He must have mistaken her for someone else. Maybe it was dawning on him because he stared down at her through narrowed eyes as if determining if he should trust her. He moved his palm slightly.

She could have screamed. But he could still shoot her before help arrived. And then he could shoot whoever might have been chivalrous enough to help her. So she spoke quietly instead. "Who do you think I am?"

His mouth curved into a slight smile. "You're Claire Molenski."

Her pulse quickened before she reminded herself that she had given him her first name. And he'd had time while she was unconscious to go through her purse and find her license. Oh, God, if he had seen her license, he also knew where she lived. He could have taken her keys, too, for her car and her house.

But why?

"Who are you?" she asked.

During their speed dating round, he had only given her his first name but that might have been as made up as his other wild stories.

"Ash," he said. "Special Agent Ash Stryker."

That name definitely sounded made up to her. But then he tugged on the chain that disappeared beneath the neck of his black sweater and pulled out a big shield. She had seen enough of those the past several years that she realized the shield was real.

And so was Special Agent Ash Stryker.

Dread overwhelmed her and she groaned. "No..."

Triumph flashed in his light blue eyes. "You didn't think we would trace the online auction back to you?"

"Online auction?" He might have been telling the truth about who he was and what had happened, but none of it made any sense to her. All she understood was that somehow her life was turning upside down—again. And she didn't know how to turn it right side up. "What do you think I'm selling?"

He just stared at her, obviously convinced that she knew, so that he wasn't even going to bother to answer.

Annoyance flashed through her. She had been too

young before to fight for herself. She wasn't going to go down this time without a fight.

"Do you think I'm selling my body?" she asked.

His lips quirked again, as if he was tempted to grin. "That might explain the speed dating and the hotel room…"

He flicked his gaze down her short, tight dress, as if he were actually considering buying. And heat flashed through her now, making her skin tingle with excitement. But then she reminded herself that he was an FBI agent, and a cold chill chased away the heat.

"But an FBI agent," she said, "*especially* an FBI special agent wouldn't waste his time investigating something that a vice cop would handle."

He arched a dark brow and asked, "Do you know much about Vice?"

"No." She sighed. "But I do know about the Federal Bureau of Investigations."

He didn't ask why; he would have read her file. The FBI probably had a volume on her by now.

"So, Special Agent Ash Stryker," she addressed him. "How are you going to ruin my life this time?"

Chapter Three

The woman was trouble. Ash had known that before he'd even met her. But she was even more dangerous in person than he had expected her to be.

Because he hadn't expected his reaction to her—his very physical, very male reaction to her beauty. Her skin was porcelain—all pale and smooth—and too much of it showed beneath the short skirt of her tight red dress. Damn, she was sexy. She knew it, too, and was using it to her advantage with that flirtatious comment about selling her body.

Hell, if she was really selling, he might have been tempted to make an offer. She was that beautiful. But she was also that treacherous.

"I have never met you before," he reminded her. "So I have had no part in ruining your life."

Was that why she had betrayed her country? Out of spite over her arrest years ago?

"You're such a *suit*," she uttered the slang word for FBI agent with total disdain. "Even without the suit, I should have realized you were an FBI agent. I knew something wasn't right with you."

Her remark had his pride stinging. He was good at going undercover. Nobody else had ever suspected he wasn't who he was pretending to be—even when he'd gone deep undercover with motorcycle gangs and militia groups. But maybe he had been more out of his element speed dating than he had ever been anywhere else.

"Actually, everything's right with me," he said. "You're the one in the wrong."

She shook her head, and her silky blond hair skimmed across her shoulders, which were bare but for thin red spaghetti straps. "I haven't done anything wrong."

"I believe that's what you said last time—"

"It was true last time, too," she insisted.

"You hacked into a bank," he reminded her since she seemed to have forgotten what she'd done. "And cleaned out someone's account."

She defensively crossed her arms over her chest. "I had my reasons."

"Do you have reasons this time, too?" he asked. "Because the only one I can think of is greed."

"You thought that was my reason last time, too," she murmured with even more disdain—as if she thought him an idiot. "But I didn't keep that money. I gave it all away to charity."

"It wasn't your money to give," he pointed out. "And *I* didn't have anything to do with your last arrest." He hadn't even been an agent then. He had probably still been a marine at that time. The Bureau had recruited him out of the service to become an agent. He had been surprised that either of them—the marines or the Bureau—had wanted him, given his background.

She sucked in a sharp breath, and her eyes widened with fear again. When she'd regained consciousness, she had seemed genuinely afraid. Despite what she'd started with her online activity, she obviously hadn't expected that she'd put herself in danger.

"Last arrest?" she repeated his words. "Is there going to be *another* arrest?"

Not unless he could find some more concrete evidence against her. It wasn't enough that knowledge only she possessed had been offered for sale. She was smart enough now that the online auction couldn't be traced directly back to her…except for that knowledge. He would have only been able to arrest her if he could have caught her in the act of selling the information. That was why he had come to the speed dating event, to pose as a buyer.

But somehow he must have spooked her before he had even been able to put in his bid. Then having to rescue her in the parking lot had completely blown his cover. Now it would be harder to find evidence against her. Now that she knew the FBI was on to her she was going to be even more careful. But maybe he could convince her to confess—if he could bluff enough that she thought the Bureau already had enough evidence for an arrest.

"You tell me if I should take you into custody," he suggested. "Have you already sold it?"

"Sold what?" she asked, acting as confused as she had when he had mentioned her online auction earlier.

Claire Molenski was as good an actress as she was a hacker because he was almost starting to buy her act. But only almost. From going undercover himself, he knew how easy it was to assume a role. He usually had to assume one of guilt because he was acting like a criminal. She was assuming one of innocence because she was acting like a victim. As if she had been unjustly persecuted before and now.

But it was just an act. Just an act…

Someone's phone rang. It wasn't his; he always kept that on vibrate. So he reached for her purse and pulled out her ringing cell.

"Maybe this is your buyer."

And maybe here was his evidence. If this caller made an offer for her information and arrangements for an exchange, Ash had her. Instead of triumph, though, he felt a flash of disappointment.

CLAIRE DIDN'T CARE that he had a gun. She grabbed for her phone anyway. She wasn't worried about him intercepting a call from a buyer. She still had no idea what he thought she was trying to sell. She was actually worried that he might intercept a call from someone from the dating service she had joined.

She didn't want a man answering her phone and scaring away a potential match. She had spent too much of her life alone; she wanted to share it with someone now.

But he ignored her attempt to grab for it and clicked on the talk button. "Hello."

She groaned. She had only given out her number to a couple of promising prospects from the dating service—to guys that the service had matched her with for compatibility. She hadn't needed five minutes or a dating service personality test to determine that she was totally incompatible with this man.

These potential matches wouldn't be too promising either after Ash got through with them, especially when he continued speaking, "This is Special Agent Stryker…"

She swallowed another groan. Uttering it would do her no good—just as explaining her hacking nine years ago had done her no good, either. She had still been arrested. She'd been convicted. She'd been sentenced. While she hadn't spent any time actually behind bars in the juvenile detention center with which she'd been threatened, she had been locked up—in a classroom studying to be an even better hacker. And then in a business that specialized in internet security.

"It's your boss," Stryker told her.

She'd worked for Peter Nowak for years, but the former CIA agent still intimidated the hell out of her. Her hand trembled slightly as she reached out for the phone, but Ash Stryker ignored her and continued to listen.

"Give it to me," she insisted.

But he shook his head, still denying her access. To her phone or to the help she would be able to seek with it? She wasn't sure how much help Peter would be, though, if he also suspected her of whatever the FBI did.

She could call a lawyer, though, like she should have last time. But she hadn't wanted her father to go broke trying to pay her legal fees.

Ash replied to whatever her boss had said with "We'll be right there." Then he clicked off her cell phone and pocketed it.

"Why are you speaking for me?" she asked. "Am I in your custody?" Had she already been arrested but she had been too drugged to understand her rights? She really needed to call a lawyer this time.

"Your boss said the building was broken into—"

She shook her head, not buying this story of his just as she hadn't the first stories he'd told her. "We have an excellent security system at the office." Peter had designed it himself. "We also have armed guards. There's no way anyone got in—"

"The alarm system was compromised," he said.

She shook her head, unable to believe it. "But there are guards—"

"One of them was shot."

She gasped as her heart pounded. She saw those

guards every day as she passed them on her way in and out of the office. "No! Who? Is he all right?"

"Nowak is at the hospital with the man."

"Then we need to go there, too," she said.

"He told us to go to the company instead."

"But why would he want me to go there?" She wasn't in management. She had nothing to do with the details of running the company or the office.

"Your personal office was the only one that had been broken into," Stryker said. "We're going there right now to make sure nothing's been taken."

"My office?" She shook her head in denial. "That makes no sense."

"Someone tried grabbing you in the parking lot," he reminded her. "Since they couldn't get the information from you directly, they must have tried getting it from your office."

She wanted to scream in frustration at his stubbornness. But apparently he wasn't the only one with the wrong idea about her. "So a man was shot over something someone thinks I'm trying to sell?"

The guard was shot because of her?

She leaped up from the bed, but the aftereffects of the chloroform must have included dizziness. Feeling faint, she nearly toppled over, but he caught her.

If what he'd claimed earlier was true, he had already caught her another time that night.

"We need to go," he said.

"To the hospital—"

"Are you all right?" he asked as he held her up, his hands warm on her shoulders.

Her legs were too rubbery for her to stand without support. But she insisted, "I'm fine." Or she would be once the room stopped spinning. "I want to go check on the guard."

"Your boss said the man is in stable condition. He will be fine," he assured her. "We need to go to your office and make sure nothing's been taken."

She hadn't left anything of value to anyone else in her office. But there were things of value to her there, things she couldn't replace. And she would be of more use at the office than she would be pacing a hospital waiting room. She wasn't even sure she knew who had been wounded, but it didn't matter. She still felt somehow responsible. Why had someone broken into the company and then only into her office?

"Okay," she said and pulled away from him. Her skin tingled from where his hands had grasped her shoulders when he'd been holding her upright. She needed distance from him. "Let's go!"

"You're in an awful hurry," he said. "But then you wouldn't want someone to *steal* what you're trying to sell."

Beyond irritated with him, she gritted her teeth and replied, "I am not selling anything."

"You want me to believe you were at this hotel tonight because you really were *speed dating*?" He sounded horrified at the prospect.

Heat rushed to her face, which had probably turned as red as her dress. "I really was…"

He glanced around the hotel room. "Is that why you rented a room?"

Her face got even hotter. "I rented a room in case I'd had too much to drink." And she felt as if she had, thanks to the chloroform making her head fuzzy and her legs weak. Or maybe Agent Stryker had made her legs weak. It really wasn't fair that the FBI agent was so ridiculously good-looking. "I didn't rent a room because I thought I'd get lucky."

There had been nothing lucky about meeting Agent Stryker. And while she wanted to meet someone else, she hadn't expected much from the speed dating experience. She certainly hadn't expected to fall in love in five minutes.

On the floor next to the bed she noticed her shoes and her purse. She stepped into the uncomfortable heels. Then she grabbed up her purse and reached into the oversize bag to search for her keys. "I'll drive myself to the office."

He held up her keys; she recognized them because the rhinestone wristband attached to the chain caught the light. She'd bought the wristband key chain so she could slip it over her wrist and always have her keys accessible. Yet she kept tossing them into her bag out of habit.

"We'll take my car," he said as he walked toward the hotel room door. He didn't wait to see if she followed him. He just opened the door and stepped into the hall.

That same feeling of helplessness washed over Claire like it had nine years ago when nobody had believed her about the hacking. Or maybe they'd only cared that she had and not *why* she had.

She didn't want to ride with him. "But *my* car has the permit for the company parking lot," she said as she hurried after him.

"My car is FBI," he said. "That gives me a permit to park wherever I want."

She pulled the hotel room door shut and mouthed his words behind his back. Sure, she was acting childish, but he was just so arrogant and infuriating and...

He chuckled, so he must have somehow witnessed her juvenile behavior. Did he have eyes in the back of his head? "Are you coming?" he asked.

She wanted to say no, but since he had her keys she had no choice. Unless she hailed a cab...

Maybe she should hail a cab. And call a lawyer.

But first she had to go to the office. Had to make sure nothing had been taken. Had to try to figure out what someone had been looking for.

But he had her keys—not just to her car but to her office, too.

"Yes," she finally, reluctantly, replied.

"Come on, then," he said, as if she was a child that needed his direction and protection. "You need to stick close to me."

He had just uttered the words when a door creaked open and a dark shadow filled the hallway ahead of him. Reminded of the man accosting her in the parking lot, Claire shivered with foreboding. She glanced back at the hotel room, but she'd closed the door. And like her keys, Ash probably had the card to the room; she couldn't re-enter without it.

So she hurried up to close the distance between them. But he held out a hand to her as if shoving her back. He used his other hand to withdraw his gun from his holster. She shook her head in protest.

If he pointed that gun at some unsuspecting hotel guests, he was going to scare them to death—like he had nearly scared her when she'd awakened to find him leaning over her.

"Ash..." Maybe she should have called him Special Agent Stryker, but for some reason his first name was what had slipped out of her lips.

Regardless of what she'd called him, he lifted a finger to his lips, silencing her.

The shadow stepped through the stairwell doorway and into the hall. The shadow belonged to a man—a big man—and like Ash, he carried a gun. He pointed the barrel at Special Agent Stryker.

"FBI," Ash called out.

The man didn't care. He cocked the gun and pulled the trigger. But Ash fired, too.

Claire screamed and ducked as bullets struck the walls of the hallway, tearing through the blue-and-green-striped paper to burrow into the drywall. Or pass through into the rooms of those unsuspecting guests.

"Stay down!" Ash ordered her.

Then a bullet must have struck him because he staggered back. But he kept his body between hers and the shooter, using it to protect her as he returned fire.

She screamed again but she wasn't worried just about herself or those guests; she was worried about him. Had he been hurt badly?

Chapter Four

Ash cursed as the force of the bullet propelled him back. He nearly knocked over Claire, who stood behind him like he had directed her. Maybe he should have told her to run. But the man with the gun stood between them and the stairwell and the elevators.

She had no place to run.

Even if he passed her the key card to the hotel room, she wouldn't be safe inside the room—at least not for long. A man this big could easily knock down her door. The only way to keep her safe was to eliminate the threat to her safety.

So Ash fired again. But this was a kill shot. The big man crumpled to the carpet like the guy in the parking lot had crumpled to the asphalt.

"It's okay," Ash told her as he turned back to Claire. "It's over." For now. But how long before someone else tried to abduct her? And why?

Why not just pay what she asked for the information? Unless she was telling the truth...

She moved as if to look around him, but he used his body to block her view. She didn't need to see what he had done to protect them. But instead of moving around him, she moved toward him—her hands reaching out toward his chest.

"Are you all right?" she asked, her voice cracking with concern.

He nodded. But he wasn't entirely convinced that he was all right because he was beginning to believe her and doubt himself. She had been so concerned about the security guard and now about him. Maybe she wasn't the mercenary person he thought she was.

"But you were shot!" she exclaimed, her palms patting his chest as if she were searching for the wound.

He caught her hands and pressed them more tightly against his vest. "I'm fine."

She shook her head. "You must be hurt."

"The protective vest took the bullet," he assured her. He had only felt the impact of the too-close shot. And he would probably have a bruise on his chest from the force with which the bullet had struck the vest. He pulled her hands away from his chest, and she tugged them free of his grasp.

"Thank God you're wearing a vest." Her breath shuddered out with sincere-sounding relief. "But of course you would be wearing a vest."

"Of course." But there had been times that he hadn't been able to when he'd been undercover. He couldn't have risked someone noticing the vest, no matter how thin and indiscernible the Bureau vests were. He also hadn't been able to wear a wire then, either. He had been totally on his own. But that hadn't been anything new to Ash.

"Maybe I should be wearing one, too," she mused, and she must have finally caught sight of the man he'd shot because she shuddered in revulsion.

"He wasn't shooting at you," he said.

Her green eyes widened in skepticism. "Really? I was right behind you."

"He wouldn't have hit you." The guy had been aiming only for Ash.

"Why not?" she asked.

"You're too valuable."

She laughed like he'd heard her laugh during the speed dating event, like he had told her a not-so-funny joke like those other guys must have. "Yeah, right…"

Was her self-deprecation real or feigned? He believed it was real, because he was beginning to believe her. He had conceived his opinion of her from her file—from the things she'd done in her past. He of all people should have known better than to think a person's past defined the kind of person he or she would become.

"The information you have is valuable," he clarified. "They want to know what you know."

"But you think I'm offering that information for sale," she said. "So why wouldn't they just pay me for it?"

"Some people would rather get the information for free," he said.

She glanced toward the man lying on the floor and shook her head. "That's not free."

No. Like the man in the parking lot, this guy had undoubtedly been hired to abduct Claire, but whatever they'd been paid hadn't been enough. The mission had cost them both their lives.

Ash rubbed his chest where the bullet had struck the vest right over his heart. If not for the vest…

During his years with the Bureau, Ash had had some dangerous assignments, but now he wondered if this mission would be the one that cost him his life.

HE HAD KILLED a man, but the police hadn't questioned him. Of course Special Agent Ash Stryker hadn't stuck around to talk to them, either. He'd whisked Claire out of the hotel as if nothing had happened.

But the gunshots still rang in her ears, and she trembled in the aftermath of the close call. Maybe he was right. Maybe the man hadn't been shooting at her. But she'd thought Ash had been hit, which had been entirely too close for her.

She had actually touched him, just to check his chest to see if a bullet had struck his heart. But he'd been wearing a vest. She'd felt the hardness beneath the softness of his sweater. Maybe she should have checked beneath the vest, too. At the thought of pulling up his sweater and peeling off that vest, her pulse quickened. Would his chest have dark hair that would be soft to her touch? Or would his muscles be all sleek and smooth beneath her palms? Her breath caught at both images.

"Is something missing?" Agent Stryker asked.

Her face heated with embarrassment that he had caught her daydreaming about him when she was supposed to be checking her ransacked office to see what could have been missing. Why would someone break into her office?

The power was on her computer but her files were untouched. Nobody would have been able to bypass her security passwords, though. And once they'd sounded the alarm and shot the guard, they wouldn't have had time to even try to figure it out.

What were they so desperate to steal from her?

She reached for the snow globe paperweight that sat next to her monitor. She shook it and watched the flakes float onto the pond, a tiny figurine of a father skated around with the tiny figurine of his daughter perched high upon his shoulders. Her breath shuddered out in relief. "It's okay."

"You were worried about a paperweight?" he asked, his blue eyes narrowed with skepticism.

"Have you ever seen anything like it?" she asked as she held it out toward him.

He shrugged. "It's a snow globe."

"It's special," she said with a soft sigh as sweet, old memories rushed over her. "My father gave it to me."

"Is he dead?"

She gasped at the horror of such a loss. "No!"

He reached for the paperweight, engulfing the delicate glass globe in his big hands. "I don't see what's so special about it," he said as he studied it more closely, "unless you hid a flash drive inside it."

Afraid that he might smash it onto the floor to look for something hidden inside, she grabbed for it, her fingers sliding over his as he gripped the globe. "Don't break it! My father had that specially made for me." To commemorate a perfect day. Of course it had been just the two of them…

Maybe she shouldn't have gotten so upset when her mother left them since she had never really spent that much time with them anyway. And Claire probably wouldn't have if her father hadn't gotten so upset. He had been in so much pain that she'd had to lash out. She sighed again, but this time with regret.

"He's not dead," Ash reminded her.

"Does he have to be?" she asked. "Why can't something he gave me be important to me while he's alive?"

Ash just shrugged again.

Her heart sank as she had a grim realization. "Your father's dead."

He jerked his head in a quick nod, as if he was embarrassed to admit it.

"I'm sorry."

Now he shrugged off her sympathy. "It happened a long time ago."

She doubted that would have lessened his pain very much. If something happened to her father, she would miss him forever. "That must have been tough on you and your mom."

"My mom died with him," he said.

Her hands still covered his, over the snow globe, so she squeezed, offering sympathy and comfort. "That must have been horrible for you. To lose them both…"

For a while she had felt like she had, too.

Ash focused on her now, as if he'd picked up on the tone of her voice. "You lost your mom."

"Yes," she said but then hastened to add, "but not like you did, though. She's alive. She's just gone. When I was sixteen, she left my dad and went to live in England with a man she'd met online."

His eyes widened, and then he nodded with sudden realization. "That was when you hacked into that bank."

"It was the bank that he used and the only money I took was from his account," she said. For some reason she wanted him to know that greed hadn't motivated her. But was it any better that spite had?

He chuckled. "And if I remember right from what I read in your file, you donated that money to a charity called Family First."

She couldn't chuckle. Even after all these years, she was still kind of bitter. Probably too bitter. "I wanted to hurt him."

"Instead you're the one you hurt," he said. "Because he pressed charges."

And yet her mother had stayed with the man. Clearly Bonita Molenski had made her choice when she'd left them, but still it had hurt Claire that her mother had cared so little about her that she would have let her go to juvenile detention. But then the FBI had offered Claire another option.

"You've definitely read my file," she mused. Either he'd read it a few times, or he had a photographic memory. She glanced around her ransacked office. "It hasn't been all bad, though. I actually enjoy what I do."

"You do?" he asked doubtfully, as if he couldn't understand why.

She laughed at his skepticism. "Yes, I do. I've not only been given permission to hack, I've been encouraged to do it. It's fun."

Or it had been until she had realized that her job was pretty much all she had. Of course she'd spent time with her dad when she hadn't been working. But he was finally over her mother and had moved on, so it was time she did the same. That was why she'd joined the dating service—one she'd trusted to make sure that none of the participants were already married like her mother had been. That hadn't been the case at the speed dating event, though. But maybe, like Ash, some of the others hadn't been there to date, either.

He sighed and released the snow globe to her hands. "You're not selling a flash drive with inside information on how to get around security firewalls."

So that was what he'd thought she was selling. "I would never sell that kind of information," she assured him.

After her arrest all those years ago, she had learned to control her impulsiveness and consider the consequences of her actions before she acted. Ironically, learning that had actually made her a better hacker.

Knuckles rapped against the glass wall of her office. "Hey, Boss, what happened here tonight?"

She turned her attention to her young assistant, who leaned now in her open doorway. His bleached white-blond hair was all mussed up as if he'd been sleeping and his eyes were red-rimmed as if he'd been out partying before he'd fallen asleep. Maybe Martin Crouch wasn't as young as she thought—he just dressed and acted young. Peter Nowak must have called him in to help her look through her ransacked office.

"The building was broken into and Harold was injured," she said. As soon as they had arrived at the company, she'd learned the name of the injured guard. Ash had checked in with the hospital again and had assured her that Harold was out of surgery and in stable condition. Fortunately, he would fully recover.

"Is—is he going to be okay?" Martin asked.

He must have been as shocked and horrified as she was. Despite checking security for banks and the government, the company had always been safe and secure—probably because most people didn't realize exactly what kind of computer consulting they did.

"Yes, he is," Ash answered for her.

Martin turned his attention to Ash and asked, "Are you a police officer?"

Claire opened her mouth, but before she could reply, Ash answered for her again. "I'm Claire's boyfriend."

She sucked in a breath of shock at his outrageous claim. Nobody would actually believe that they were dating—not a former lawbreaker and an FBI agent. But maybe Ash didn't intend to tell anyone that he was an agent. Her boss knew but national security relied on his ability to keep secrets.

Martin's bleached blond brows arched in surprise. As her assistant, he knew how many hours they worked and how little time she had for a relationship. "Really?"

"We met through a dating service," Ash replied with a pointed stare at her—probably so that she would back his story.

"Really?" Martin asked again, and he turned toward Claire now.

Technically Ash hadn't lied, but she wondered why he hadn't told more of the truth. Like what he really did for a living. Could he suspect Martin of being involved in offering that information for sale? He suspected her, though, and had revealed that he was an FBI agent. But maybe he'd only done that because she'd nearly been abducted.

Aware of the danger, she followed his lead and replied, "Yes, really. Ash and I met at a speed dating event." Like Ash, she left out the part that it had been just that evening.

"How come you didn't mention anything to me about meeting someone?" Martin asked, sounding hurt, which surprised her.

He was her assistant but not her confidant. She didn't share everything with him. She lifted her shoulders in a slight shrug. "I wanted to see how it worked out before I said anything."

She was damn sure a relationship would never work out between her and the FBI agent. He thought she was a criminal, and she thought he was too uptight and judgmental.

"So you're okay?" Martin asked. At first she wasn't sure what he was talking about—her and Ash—or the break-in. But then he added, "Nothing was taken?"

She tightly clasped the snow globe and shook her head. "Nothing."

"That's good," he said. "Do you want me to help you clean up?"

"No, but thanks for asking, Martin." She was surprised

that he had, though, because she rarely let him touch anything in her space even though he was her assistant.

She hated that someone else had been in her office, touching her things, moving and throwing them around the small area. She didn't need everything to be neat; she just needed it to be where she'd left it so she would know where to find it again. At least they hadn't broken the globe or, as far as she could tell, anything else.

"It's so late," she told Martin, "that you should just go home." Like she just wanted to go home...

Martin glanced to Ash again. Either he was concerned about leaving her alone with this strange man or he was seeking permission from Ash to leave.

He was her assistant, though. He was supposed to defer to her. Usually he did—when he wasn't preoccupied with whatever games he was playing when he should be working instead.

Ash assured him, "I'll take care of her."

Was he offering that assurance as an FBI agent? Or as the boyfriend he was pretending to be?

Easily accepting Ash's claim, Martin nodded and headed for the door. He was probably eager to go back to bed. Or maybe to the party...

Ash waited until her assistant was out of earshot before he asked her, "There really is nothing missing? Not even a flash drive?"

She glanced at the contents of her open desk drawer before closing it again. It had been a long night. She should have been tired, too. "Maybe a flash drive..."

He tensed, his spine straightening so that he stood even taller, making him even more imposing since the muscles in his arms stretched the sleeves of his sweater. His jaw was rigid with tension. He was an FBI agent on full alert.

She laughed at his overreaction and couldn't resist teasing him. "It's okay. I have those photos on my hard drive at home. I don't think the thieves are going to find them nearly as special as I do, though."

He didn't laugh; he didn't even smile. His handsome face still tense, he asked, "Personal photos?"

A pang of panic struck her heart as a terrifying thought occurred to her. "You don't think they'll use those photos to go after my family?"

After all, those men had been so determined to abduct her that they had given up their own lives. In order to get to her, they might use someone close to her to influence her. Could what she did for a living actually put her father and his bride at risk?

Chapter Five

Ash didn't offer Claire false reassurance because it was possible that someone might use her family as leverage to get her to reveal her secrets. And if he continued being honest with her, she might begin to trust him enough to tell him everything she knew. Because even though he now believed she hadn't offered that security information for sale, she probably knew who might have.

Could her assistant have had something to do with it? He hadn't looked bright or mature enough to come up with such a plan, though. But then Claire had only been sixteen when she'd hacked into that bank system.

"Tell me about your assistant," he said even though he already had checked out everyone who worked for Nowak Computer Consulting. That was how Claire Molenski had become his main suspect.

She glanced up from straightening her desk and laughed. "You can't seriously suspect Martin of anything?"

"He's your assistant," he said. "So he must work closely with you, checking security on the same high target sites that you do."

She gestured around her small office. There was only one desk and only one chair. "I work alone."

Nowak Computer Consulting was the only company

who'd had access to all the sites that had been offered up for sale at the online auction. So Ash had thoroughly studied it. As well as talking to Peter Nowak, he had scrutinized the building floor plans and scoured security footage. He knew the layout probably better than Claire did. Just a few steps from her office was the bull pen of cubicles where the assistants worked.

"But he's your assistant, so doesn't he assist you with the projects you're working on?" he asked. Company protocol claimed otherwise, but Ash knew people whose assistants did more of the work than they did.

"No," she corrected him. "As my assistant, Martin brings me coffee and lunch and dinner, if I'm working late." She sighed. "Which I usually am."

Maybe Ash had made too many assumptions about Claire Molenski—although he hadn't been wrong about how much time she spent at the consulting company. He'd thought it was because she legally had to, but maybe it was also because she wanted to. "He doesn't help you with any of your projects?"

"He helps with whatever tasks I give him to handle," she said. "But he doesn't have the clearance to work most of the projects I work."

Because she had the highest clearance at the company. Peter Nowak had reluctantly admitted that to Ash when he'd interviewed the man. The former CIA agent trusted his star hacker, but Ash trusted no one. That was why Claire Molenski was his number-one suspect.

SHE WAS HIS number one-suspect—of whatever he suspected her. The suspicion was back in his piercing blue eyes as he stared at her. She hadn't helped herself by defending Martin. But there was no way her assistant could be guilty of anything that had people getting shot at and killed.

"Who does have the clearance level you have or an even higher level?" he asked.

"My boss." Peter Nowak had been a CIA agent before he'd started his computer consultation business, though. That was why some of the biggest banks and financial institutions in the world as well as the US and several other governments had entrusted him to ensure their internet security. He was good at what he did, and he was beyond suspicion.

So she wasn't surprised when Agent Ash Stryker didn't even blink those surprisingly long, black lashes of his. He had no suspicions about Peter Nowak. His suspicions were all about her.

"None of the other hackers have your level of clearance?" he asked.

Maybe he was willing to consider another suspect. But she didn't have anyone to offer him.

"I don't know," she said. "But I suspect that you know."

"You," he said, confirming her fears. "You have the highest clearance besides Peter Nowak."

She sighed as weariness overwhelmed her. It had been a long day before someone had tried abducting her from the parking lot of the speed dating hotel. "I thought so." That was why she worked so many hours—nobody else could work on the projects she worked. "Since Leslie retired…"

"Leslie?"

"Leslie Morrison retired last year. I was his assistant when I first started working here," she explained. "Leslie taught me everything I know, a lot more than I learned in college." Her professors had been behind the new technology, while Mr. Nowak's company had been beyond it—far beyond it.

"So Leslie is a better hacker than you are?"

She shivered at his coldly suspicious tone. She hadn't offered up Leslie to defray guilt from herself. She wasn't guilty, and neither was Leslie. She slammed her desk drawer shut. "Leslie isn't a hacker anymore."

"I'm sure he still knows how to hack, though," Agent Stryker persisted.

She shook her head. "Hacking isn't like riding a bike. Technology changes so quickly that you have to constantly be hacking to be any good. If you're away from it too long, you're going to be so far behind the security systems and software that you won't be able to hack into anything anymore."

And she'd done it again—deflected guilt off someone else and back onto herself. He was looking at her that way again, as if he was imagining himself slapping cuffs on her, while just a short while ago she'd been imagining herself undressing him.

It really was unfair that he was so good-looking. The FBI agents who had arrested her the first time had been old, or at least they had seemed old to her sixteen-year-old self. Their hair had been gray and receding while their waistlines had been expanding.

Why couldn't Ash Stryker look like that?

Why did his black hair have to be so thick and soft looking? So soft looking that she was tempted to run her fingers through it...

She had been right to join the dating service. It had been entirely too long since she'd been with a man. That had to be the reason why she was so physically attracted to Ash. It had to be the only reason.

"Are you done here?" he asked.

She glanced around the small office. She had organized it again—as much as it was ever organized. It didn't look neat, but at least things were back where she had left them. She shuddered at the thought of someone touching all her stuff. Had they touched her globe, too? If not the intruders, the crime lab who'd investigated and collected evidence might have. They'd left fingerprint dust all over, too, which she'd had to clean up. She hated cleaning.

She reached for the globe again, tempted to take it home with her. But she wasn't sure she was going home. And with security increased at the company, nobody would ever be able to break in again. The globe would be safe. But was she?

"What if I tell you that I am done?" she asked. "Will you take me back to the hotel to get my car?"

"No," he said, and his deep voice held that no-nonsense, matter-of-fact tone that so infuriated her.

His reply confirmed her suspicion that he was actually going to bring her in for questioning. He might even arrest her. She didn't understand exactly what crime he suspected her of, but she had offered him no other suspects.

She drew in a deep breath and stood, ready for him to slap the cuffs on her, ready to relive all her nightmares from nine years ago...

IT WAS LATE.

Too late to question her any further. So Ash wasn't taking her back to the Bureau. For one, he was beginning to believe she really didn't know any more than she'd already told him. And secondly, she was exhausted.

Her slight body slumped down in the passenger's seat of his Bureau-issued black SUV. She was nearly asleep, but she fought back a yawn and told him, "You didn't have to drive me home."

He heard the surprise in her voice; she hadn't expected him to bring her home. She had suspected him to arrest her. Earlier that evening, he would have thought that was because she had a guilty conscience. But now that he was beginning to get to know her better...

He wasn't sure what to think of Claire Molenski anymore. She was smart, but he'd already known that. She was sexy; that he hadn't known. He hadn't known how his body would react to hers. While she shivered slightly despite the heat blowing out of the vents, his skin was hot, his body tense.

That could have been just because of the adrenaline. He had nearly lost her a couple of times. He had to be vigilant because it wasn't a question of if there would be another attempt to grab her. It was a question of when.

And that made him wonder about her guilt.

Maybe her only crime was being too smart. But then who had offered her knowledge for sale? He had been so certain she was the threat that he hadn't really considered other suspects. Only Nowak Computer Consulting, or "No Hack" as it was known in inner circles, had the means to infiltrate those sites.

"You could have just brought me back to my car at the hotel," she said.

He could have. Or he could have handed her off to another agent to drive home. He didn't do security detail. His specialty had always been putting himself at risk, going undercover rather than protecting other people.

"No, I couldn't," he said. While he worked with good agents, damn good agents, he hadn't wanted to trust anyone else with her safety. "There have already been two attempts to abduct you." He suspected there would be more—many more—since so many radical groups and subversive governments wanted the information she possessed.

"Me," she murmured.

"Yes, you." They hadn't been after him…except to kill him and get him out of their way.

"They were after me," she said, as if she were strangely trying to reassure herself of that fact. Then he understood her reasoning when she added, "So Dad and Pam will be safe…"

"Pam?"

"She's my dad's new wife," Claire explained. "And a very sweet lady. Like my dad, she was a single parent for years, so she never had enough money to travel. Because of that they're taking a long honeymoon to visit all the places they've always wanted to see. They won't be home for months."

She jerked her head in a sharp nod. "So that's good. They'll be safe…"

Even as his focus stayed on the road, checking for a tail, he could feel her gaze on him. But again he wouldn't offer her any false reassurance. He would leave that to her. It sounded as if she was doing a good job of convincing herself that her loved ones weren't in danger because of her.

But then she sighed and admitted, "But someone could still track their credit cards." Now she played her own devil's advocate. "They could pull up their travel itinerary and find them—"

"I'll put a protective detail on them," he offered as he steered the SUV into the lot of her apartment complex. "We'll make sure they're safe."

She reached across the console, grasped his arm and

squeezed. "Thank you. But they're not even in the country right now."

"It's okay," he said. "No matter where they are, we can still protect them." At the moment he was more concerned about her safety, though. Ever since he had suspected that she was the threat to national security, he'd had a detail on her apartment, so it should be safe.

But several agents had been watching her earlier that evening, and she had been drugged and nearly abducted...

He worried that she may not be safe anywhere. While the only security he specialized in was national security, he would do his best to keep her and her family safe.

She breathed a heavy sigh of relief. "Thank you for protecting them. They deserve to be happy."

"What about you?" he asked, as he turned off the engine.

When he had been thinking like an FBI agent, he had only been concerned about her professional life. Now he was thinking like a man around her, and he wondered about her personal life. He hadn't missed her assistant's shock that she might have a boyfriend.

Didn't she date very often?

When had he had his last date? He couldn't remember one where he'd been himself and not undercover and just dating for information.

"What about me?" she asked. The lights had shut off inside the SUV, but in the dim glow of the parking lamps, he could see her pale brow furrow in confusion.

He turned fully toward her. Despite the console between the bucket seats, they were close. And with her fingers clenching his forearm, they were touching. He stared into her face, into her eyes that sparkled in the shadows. And he asked, "Do you deserve to be happy?"

She snatched back her hand from his arm and turned away from him. As she pushed open the passenger's door, she replied, "I served my sentence."

He wondered now if that had been too harsh. "I'm not talking about that," he said as he hurried around the SUV to her side.

To protect her...

He glanced around the dimly lit parking lot as he led her toward the door to the building that housed her unit. There were several buildings in the complex. And in that building there were several floors, several apartments. Someone could have slipped past that security detail he had on her place. He shouldn't have brought her back here.

"What are you talking about?" she asked as she dug inside that mammoth bag of hers for the keys that he pulled from his pocket. She took the ring from his hand and quickly found the key that opened the door to the lobby. It was nothing fancy—worn terrazzo floors and chipped plaster walls. But it was close to her office. He wondered if that was why she'd chosen to live here.

He waited until they stepped inside the elevator before he replied to her question. "I was just wondering if you are..."

She arched a blond brow. "Are what?"

"Happy."

She leaned wearily against the mirrored wall of the elevator. The image of her in that tight, sexy red dress reflected around him as if she were surrounding him. Ash struggled to draw a deep breath when he felt like panting as his pulse quickened.

"I thought I was," she said. "Until I saw how happy my dad and Pam are."

Now he knew why she had been at that speed dating

event and it hadn't been to sell security secrets as he had suspected. She had posted online that she would be there, which he'd thought was her way of opening the bidding for information. But she had actually been there to find her happiness. She had really wanted to meet someone and she didn't need to tell him for him to know that she hadn't been looking for him. It was clear that after that arrest in her teens she didn't have any trust or affection for FBI agents.

Not that he could have dated her had she been interested in him. He had no time for a personal life and no inclination to make time, either.

The elevator was old, but it was fast and came quickly to a stop on the fifth floor. He breathed a slight sigh of relief that it had saved him from having to comment on her statement.

She stepped out of the elevator and headed down the dimly lit hall. Uneasy, Ash pulled his gun from his holster as he walked beside her. And when she stopped and extended the key toward the lock on her door, he covered her hand with his to turn the knob.

She glanced up at him, her green eyes wide with sudden curiosity. And she asked, "Are you?"

"Am I what?" he said, distracted by her closeness and by that uneasy feeling that he hadn't had enough agents watching her apartment.

Her mouth turned up slightly at the corners as she replied, "Happy…"

Instead of answering her question, he pushed open the door. Then he pushed her behind him for protection as he saw the total devastation. It was worse than her office had been.

And he worried that whoever had searched her place was still inside—waiting for her.

Chapter Six

Her heart pounded quickly with fear as the FBI agent pointed his gun inside her apartment.

"Stay back," Ash directed her like he had in the hotel hallway. He had been right then: there had been a threat—a man with a gun who'd shot at him.

But she heard no shots now, so she peered around him. "What's wrong?"

"Someone broke into your place."

Even though the heat and strength of his hand covering hers had distracted her, she'd felt the lock turn as the key had disengaged the dead bolt. She glanced at the door frame. It was old with paint peeling, but it wasn't damaged beyond normal wear and tear. "Nobody broke in."

"But it's been ransacked."

Heat rushed to her face with a tide of embarrassment. "No. It already looked this way…"

Except that she hadn't noticed before how messy it was until she saw her place now through his eyes. She had left clothes and books and junk mail strewn all over the furniture and even the floor.

"It did?" he asked. He seemed horrified.

Not only was he an all-too-serious FBI agent, he was probably also a neat freak. If he had actually been at the speed dating event to meet a potential match, it wouldn't have been her. They had nothing in common. So it was probably good that he had only been there to stop her from betraying her country. His thinking her capable of treason was yet another reason they were not at all compatible.

"With as much as I work, I don't have time to clean," she said in defense of her mess.

"You could hire a cleaning lady," he suggested as he reholstered his gun.

But then she'd have someone touching her stuff, putting it away so she'd have to look for it. She leaned down to pick up some clothes from the floor and, like she had at the hotel, she mouthed the words back at him. And as she straightened up again, she saw the grin on his face reflecting back from the glass of her darkened window.

He must have caught her. Again.

"It's not like I spend a lot of time here," she said and flinched at the defensiveness in her voice. She didn't have to make excuses to him. It was none of his business how messy her apartment was.

"So shouldn't it be cleaner, then?" he remarked, his blue eyes twinkling with amusement. At her expense.

She tossed the armload of clothes at him. But his reflexes were quick and he dodged all but the black lace bra that draped over his shoulder. He hooked his finger into the strap and held it up between them as he teased, "Couldn't make it to the bedroom?"

Her face heated even more so that it was probably more maroon than red now as her embarrassment and anger increased.

"You really want to think the worst of me," she said. "You want to think that I'm a hacker and a wh—"

He moved quickly—so quickly that he pressed a finger

over her lips before she could utter the ugly word. "I never called you that," he said.

His gaze skimmed down her body. Now her skin heated and tingled all over—just from how he looked at her. What if he actually touched her?

Of course it had nothing to do with him. Personally. She was probably just unnerved because it had been so long since she'd dressed like this, since she had even attempted to have a social life. She wasn't sure she knew how to anymore. The last time she'd dated she had been a teenager. Then there had been that one boy in college. But he'd been a boy.

There had never been a man.

And Ash Stryker was definitely a man. He wasn't her type at all. But…

She stepped back, so that his hand fell away from her mouth. "I'm not selling anything," she said.

"I know," he replied, sounding almost regretful.

Had he wanted her to be the hacker or had he wanted her…? That was unlikely—especially after he'd seen her messy apartment.

"I don't get this whole online auction thing that had you ready to arrest me," she said.

Fortunately he hadn't been as ready as she'd thought he was since he had brought her home instead of to jail. But then he would have needed evidence to arrest her, and he wouldn't find anything to tie her to a crime she hadn't committed. But what was the crime?

"I may have rushed to a conclusion," he reluctantly admitted.

Since he could admit that he'd been wrong, maybe he wasn't as uptight as she'd thought him. And maybe he wasn't the only one who'd made assumptions since she had been equally as quick to label him as uptight.

"Did you rush to a conclusion or a conviction?" she asked him, her pride still stinging that he'd been so quick to think her a traitor.

He sighed. "There wouldn't have been any conviction without hard evidence."

"I don't understand how there could be any evidence," she said. "I don't even understand exactly what's being offered for sale."

"A way around the firewalls," he said. "The access to secure government data could shut down the country or at least cripple it. The economy—"

"I understand that," she said. "Obviously. That's why I do what I do."

"I thought you did what you do because it was part of your sentence and probation."

"It started out that way," she conceded. "But I served out that sentence and my probation a while ago."

And now she was compensated for the work she did. She was actually compensated very well. She really could afford a cleaning lady; maybe she should hire one. Not because he had suggested it, though. She leaned over and picked up a few more things.

"What I don't understand," she continued, "is how someone thinks they could get around a firewall. Once I find the flaw in a security system, I fix it. I make it go away before anyone else has a chance to find it. That's what I do—that's what Nowak Computer Consulting does."

"Could someone have hacked into your computer and be piggybacking—"

She laughed. "*Nobody* can hack me."

"What about Leslie Morrison, your old trainer?" he asked. "If he taught you so much…"

She winced over a twinge of regret. She had cast suspicion on Leslie even though she hadn't meant to. "He's retired. I already explained to you that to be effective, you have to be active—"

"So it's not Leslie," he agreed.

The twinge of pain eased with relief that he so readily agreed with her. Leslie was happy being retired. He would not appreciate the upheaval of an FBI investigation. Had Special Agent Stryker agreed too easily though? Was he only humoring her?

"But the thing about hackers," he said, "is that there's always a better one. Maybe someone in another country…"

First he'd insulted her integrity; now he was insulting her skills. "If someone else could hack into those firewalls, why are people trying to abduct *me*?"

"I'm not the only one who thinks you're the seller," he suggested. "Someone else does, too."

"But I'm not," she said emphatically, "so what's the point of abducting me when I won't sell them any information?"

"They're trying to abduct you because they don't intend to *pay* you," he said.

Her head had begun to pound a while ago, so she pushed her fingers against her temples to relieve the pressure. "Then how do they intend to get the information? Despite what you think, I won't freely betray my country." She hastened to add, "I wouldn't have done it for money, either."

"Torture," he replied matter-of-factly as if he was quite familiar with it. Because he had been tortured? Or because he had tortured someone? "If you won't tell them freely, they will torture the information out of you."

"But there is no information anymore," she said. "I

made sure that there is no way around any of those firewalls."

"Then they'll kill you." Maybe he was only trying to scare her.

If so, his mission was accomplished. She shuddered with fear and with cold. She wanted to take a hot shower, and then she wanted to go to bed—even though her sleep would undoubtedly be interrupted with nightmares of abductions and shootings. "Well, I'm home. I'm safe. You can leave now."

She wasn't just scared; she was also exhausted. So exhausted that, earlier, she had briefly entertained some crazy thoughts about Ash Stryker. About undressing him.

If only he wasn't an FBI agent…

"You're not safe here," he told her.

Then why had he brought her home? To search it? He hadn't touched anything besides her bra, though.

"We established this is my mess," she said, gesturing around at the cluttered apartment. "Nobody broke in here. I will be fine." Maybe. Once she had a shower and some sleep. If she could sleep…

Not only was her skin tingling but her pulse was racing. She preferred to think that it was only because of the threats to her safety and not because of Ash Stryker. She couldn't be reacting to his nearness. She couldn't be reacting to him. It was just a reaction, just shock from everything that had happened that evening.

He touched his ear and she realized he was wearing some kind of undetectable radio device. "You're not safe because a suspicious vehicle just pulled into the parking lot. The agent who's been watching your apartment thinks there's at least one armed gunman." As he said it, he reached for the weapon in his holster.

"Someone must have followed us from the office," she said.

He shook his head. "Nobody followed me." He didn't sound defensive or offended—just very confident in his abilities. "They must have found your apartment address when they broke into your office."

"No," she said. "I don't keep anything with personal information on it in my office." She worked with hackers. She wasn't entirely confident that one wouldn't use whatever she might leave around to hack into her personal accounts. They probably wouldn't have done it maliciously but just to prove that they were as good as she was.

"At the moment it doesn't matter how they got here," he said. "And we're not going to stick around to ask them how, either."

"But we don't know for sure that they're here for me," she protested as he headed toward the door.

"We can't risk it in case they are," he said. "We have to get out of here."

She shivered again with fear and coldness. The evening had grown too cool for her short sleeveless dress that left her arms and legs bare. She glanced longingly at the warmer clothes scattered about the floor and furniture. Instead of hurling them at Agent Stryker, she should have put on some of them. But she hadn't known then that she would have to leave again because the danger she was in had followed her home.

ASH DIDN'T HAVE a moment to lose. The fifth-floor apartment didn't give them many escape options besides the only door. Neither of them was likely to survive a fall from one of the windows—not from this height.

He caught her wrist and tugged her into the hall behind

him. The elevator wasn't a safe option, either. "Where are the stairs?"

She entwined her fingers with his and tugged him down the hall. "This way," she said. "I usually take them."

That explained why she was so fit despite all the hours she clocked at the computer consulting company.

Then she grumbled and added, "Just not in heels."

Maybe he should have let her change, but he doubted they had time to spare. And he liked that red dress. Maybe a little too much…

She pushed open the door to the stairway. As they headed down the first flight, her heels clicked against each step and echoed off the brick walls. But there was another echo, the clang of a door opening onto the stairwell. Someone was coming up while they were going down—to cut them off?

But then whoever was coming for her wouldn't know that she had been warned of the threat. They would think she was still in her apartment—waiting to be abducted. He caught her arm and pulled her to a stop on the landing between the third and second floors. Beneath his palm her skin was like silk.

She shivered. "What—"

He pressed a finger over her lips like he had in her apartment. "Someone's coming up the stairs," he whispered.

Her eyes widened with panic as she finally heard them, too—the other footsteps echoing in the stairwell. They were heavy footsteps, which meant they were probably big men.

"What do we do?" she whispered, her lips moving against his finger.

"This," he said, and he whirled her around and pressed

her back against the brick wall of the stairwell. She gasped just as he lowered his mouth to hers.

Not only did he cover her mouth with his but he covered her body, too. To hide her. To protect her.

That had been his intent. But her lips were soft beneath his, her breath warm, and he found himself really kissing her. He moved his mouth over hers, taking advantage of her parted lips to deepen the kiss.

And her arms moved between them. Instead of pushing him away, as he expected, they linked around his neck. And she clung to him.

Maybe it was out of fear since the footsteps had grown louder. Finally a man passed them, chuckling beneath his breath. Another man muttered a comment, "Man, they can't even wait until they get to their apartment…"

He passed them, as well. The men's footsteps pounded up a couple more flights, and then a door opened and slammed shut on the fifth floor. Her floor.

Ash forced himself to pull away and then step back from Claire. But he kept his hand on her, steadying her as she trembled.

"They'll be back," he warned, "once they find your apartment empty. We have to move quickly."

But his legs were a little shaky as he headed down the stairs. Passion had nearly overwhelmed him. He'd known she was dangerous; he just hadn't realized how dangerous.

She was so sexy that she had distracted him. She had nearly made him forget why he'd kissed her in the first place—since kissing her had felt so damn right. And hot. His pulse still raced, and not because of the threat those gunmen posed.

She stumbled on the last step, and he caught her, his arms going around her again. She stared up at him, her green eyes wide with confusion. Then her pale skin flushed, and she pulled away from him and muttered a curse. "These damn heels."

"You may need to take them off if we have to run," he advised her.

She nodded in agreement.

But then her feet would be bare, and she was already shivering. Too bad he hadn't caught more than the bra from that pile of clothes she'd thrown at him. She could have used a sweater and some pants. Hell, she could have used the bra since it wasn't apparent to him that she was wearing one beneath that tight dress. But he didn't have the bra anymore, either. She'd snatched it back from him.

"Or I can carry you," he suggested. Maybe that would be best—or at least the fastest—if they needed to get away in a hurry. But instead of reaching for her, he reached for the door to the lobby and pushed it open just enough so that he could glimpse outside the stairwell.

Had the gunmen left another man in the lobby in case she managed to escape them? The agents watching her building from the parking lot hadn't been certain how many gunmen there were. Two or three? And they hadn't wanted to storm the building and risk a shoot-out that could endanger other residents.

Despite the late hour, the lobby wasn't deserted. A man paced the worn terrazzo tile. He was tall and muscular, and as he paced, his black leather jacket fell open, revealing the holster and the gun he wore beneath it.

As she tried to peer over his shoulder, Claire pressed against Ash's back, and her closeness warmed his blood and quickened his pulse. She gasped and her warm breath tickled his ear.

"We're trapped," she whispered. "There's a guy out there and those two guys upstairs."

He turned his head, and his lips nearly brushed hers since she was so close to him. He could still taste her sweetness, but he wanted to kiss her again. Hell, he wanted to do a lot more than kiss her.

"Where are we going to go?" she asked. "How are we going to get away?"

"Don't worry," he said. "I'll protect you." But then who was going to protect him—from her?

She sucked in a breath as her eyes widened more with fear. "Oh, no, it's too late…"

That was what he was afraid of—that it was already too late for him to protect himself from Claire Molenski. She was getting to him in a way that no one else ever had.

Her body trembled against his. "He's seen us," she said. "He's coming for us."

But Ash didn't even reach for his gun. As she'd said, it was too late.

Chapter Seven

If Ash wouldn't draw his weapon, Claire would. But when she reached for his holster, he caught her fingers. His big hand completely engulfed hers. She tried to tug free, but he held on to her as he opened the door to the armed gunman who'd been pacing the lobby.

"What the hell were you doing?" the man asked. "You took your sweet time bringing her down here."

Ash was working *with* him. The guy had unruly dark hair that had gone too long without a cut, just like his darkly shadowed jaw had gone too long without a shave. Along with the leather jacket, he wore faded and torn jeans and motorcycle boots. Was Ash not really the FBI agent that he claimed to be? But then she noticed the badge dangling around this man's neck, beneath his leather jacket. He was an FBI agent, too.

She expelled a breath of relief.

"You could have given me a heads-up that they were taking the stairs, too," Ash grumbled as he pushed past the man and continued through the lobby. His hand still clasped around Claire's, he tugged her along behind him.

"I just got here," the other agent replied.

Ash stopped at the lobby door that led out into the parking lot. "Why are you here anyway, Reyes? You're Organized Crime, not Antiterrorism."

"You don't think your terrorists are the only ones who'd like to buy what she's selling?" he scoffed.

"She's not selling anything," Ash replied for her—as had become his annoying habit.

The other agent's dark brows arched in surprise. "You've convinced her not to betray our country?"

"*She* was never going to betray our country," Claire said before Ash could answer for her again. "And Agent Stryker realized he was a fool for making assumptions about Ms. Molenski's character."

Agent Reyes laughed.

But Ash's face stayed tense, his lips not even curving into a slight smile over her comments. "When they realize that her apartment is empty, they're going to come back down looking for her," he said. "We need to get out of here. Now."

The grin slid off Reyes's handsome face. Why were these FBI agents so damn good-looking? It wasn't fair.

"You get Ms. Molenski to safety," Reyes said. "I've got this."

"Alone?" Ash asked with a glance around the lobby.

Reyes shrugged. "It's better than having you stay and shoot them," he said. "Dead men can't tell us who they're working for."

"A dead agent can't ask them who they're working for," Stryker said. "I hope you have more backup." But he didn't wait around to find out; he pushed open the door and led Claire from the lobby into the parking lot.

"Shouldn't you stay?" she asked Ash. "Shouldn't you help him?"

His hand on his gun, he peered around the dimly lit lot as he led the way to the black SUV. There were a few other ones in the lot, and as he passed one, the lights on it blinked on and off. There were other FBI agents around, but Ash replied, "Reyes can take care of himself."

"So can I." She had been taking care of herself for years. And when her father had been so lost after her mom left them, she had taken care of him, too. Maybe she had taken care of him a little too well when she had tried to avenge his broken heart.

Ash stopped at the passenger's door to his SUV, and as he opened that door for her, he shook his head. "You can't. Not against people like this."

Terrorists and criminals, according to what the agents had said moments ago.

He slammed the door and then in seconds he was behind the wheel, starting the engine and turning the heat on full blast. But she couldn't stop trembling.

He was right. Even though she'd fought at the hotel, she had still been easily overpowered, drugged and abducted. If he hadn't intervened, she'd probably be undergoing torture about now—for codes, that didn't even exist, to bypass government firewalls.

He and Agent Reyes dealt with people like this every day, putting their lives in danger to protect others. She respected that, but she wanted no part of it. In her own life or in the life of the person with whom she wanted to share hers, because worrying about that person every time he went to work would be another form of torture for her.

CLAIRE HAD BEEN quiet since they'd left her apartment. She hadn't even been mouthing snarky comments behind his back. He kind of missed the snarky comments. Actually, he just missed her spirit and spunk.

Maybe she was quiet because she was completely exhausted. It had been an incredibly long, dangerous day for her.

And it probably hadn't helped that he'd started out treating her like a suspect. He hadn't been overly sensitive or respectful of what she was going through. Maybe she was quiet because she just hated his guts.

"Reyes is okay," he told her since she had seemed concerned about the offbeat agent. And as if to prove it, he turned on the two-way radio in the SUV, so that she could hear what he heard through his earpiece.

"I'm not sure they were after her," Reyes was saying. "I didn't recognize them."

"Do you know every criminal in the Chicago area?" Ash asked him.

"Pretty much," he said. "I either grew up with them or I've arrested them. Sometimes—hell, usually—it's been both."

"That must make it hard for you to maintain friendships," Ash quipped.

Yet he doubted Reyes had any trouble making or keeping friends; the man seemed to have never met a stranger...until these two men who'd been in Claire's apartment complex. Their voices hadn't betrayed any accents, but that didn't mean they couldn't be from some other country or, as mercenaries, were representing the interests of some other country.

"At least none of them have burned down *my* house," Reyes teased in reference to Ash's comments about arresting his childhood friends.

"It would be a little hard for them to do that from behind bars. And it's not like Blaine lit the match himself," Ash defended his friend. He and Blaine Campbell's friendship didn't go back to childhood, but it went back to the marines where they had forged an unbreakable bond. That was why he'd been letting his friend stay at his place when he'd been on another undercover assignment.

"True, he didn't light the match," Reyes agreed. "But he was too distracted to smell the fire and put it out."

"The fire was the least of his concerns," Ash said. Blaine had put himself on security duty, protecting the witness from the bank robberies Blaine had been trying to solve. He had nearly lost her and his own life in that fire.

"Exactly. That's why he was distracted and nearly got killed," Reyes said. "I hope you're not letting Ms. Molenski distract you like that."

Now he wished he hadn't turned on the radio in the SUV. "You know me," he said. He had worked with Reyes before, even before they had helped Blaine with the bank robbers. They had worked so well together that they had actually become friends. "You know that's not going to happen."

Ash wasn't like his friend Blaine who had grown up with three or four sisters in a house of women and liked to play hero to damsels in distress.

Ash didn't want to be anyone's hero. He never willingly did protection duty. But for some reason he felt as if no one else could protect Claire like he would, as if she actually was his girlfriend.

"I thought I knew you." Reyes chuckled. "The funny thing is that the only information I got out of those two guys was a story about some couple making out in the stairwell—"

Ash clicked off the radio before Reyes could say anything else. The other agent enjoyed joking around too much.

"Don't worry," Claire said. "I know you only kissed

me so those two guys couldn't get a look at me and possibly recognize me."

That was the reason he'd started out kissing her. It wasn't the reason that he had barely been able to stop, though.

"But now it sounds like they might not have been looking for me after all," she continued. "So I could have stayed home." Her small mouth stretched in a big yawn. "And slept."

"I'll take you somewhere you can sleep," he told her. "And you'll be able to rest assured that no one else will be coming for you. You wouldn't know that at your place. Someone must have followed you from there to the hotel, so they had known where you live even before breaking into your office."

"I went to the hotel straight from the office," she said. "That must've been how I was tracked down at the hotel. It's not like I was watching for anyone to follow me."

He was watching for a tail, his gaze divided between the rearview and side mirrors, the road in front of them and her. She kept drawing his attention. Of course he had to check on her to make sure she was okay. But that wasn't the only reason why he was drawn to her.

"But I don't know how anyone found my apartment," she said, "unless they followed us home from the office."

He sure as hell hoped not or he must have been as distracted as Reyes worried she would make him. "I'm sorry," he said.

"Why?" she asked. "For letting someone follow us?"

"No," he said. "No one followed us." Despite his attraction to her, he had been too cautious. They must have found her address another way; maybe the department of motor vehicles had been hacked and her address pulled off her license.

"Then why are you apologizing?" she asked. "For kissing me? Like I said, I understand why you did."

"I'm not apologizing for kissing you." Because it wasn't something he regretted. "I'm apologizing for making the wrong assumptions about your character."

She laughed at his repeating her words—or maybe at his actually apologizing. Honestly it wasn't something he did very often, but that was because he usually wasn't wrong.

Her laughter turned into a ragged sigh. "Unfortunately you're not the only one who made the wrong assumptions about me. How can we make these other people realize that they're wrong, too?"

"Good question," he murmured.

"Can I post a disclaimer somewhere?" she asked. "Swear that I have no secret security information for sale?"

"You could," he agreed, albeit reluctantly.

She heard the reluctance because she turned toward him and narrowed her eyes. "But you don't want me to," she surmised. "Why not?"

"Because then these people might actually find the real seller and get that information they want." Then that catastrophe he'd tried to avert might come to pass.

She shook her head. "That's not possible. I told you the information doesn't exist."

"You think it doesn't exist," he said. "But maybe you're the one making the wrong assumptions now."

She opened but then closed her mouth without uttering a word. She just shook her head.

Maybe she was protesting his comment. Or maybe she was protesting that he'd pulled the SUV into the parking lot of a hotel along the lakeshore in southern Michigan.

He had been driving for a while. She must have realized he was taking her outside the city.

Or maybe she hadn't been paying attention at all because she asked, "Where have you brought me?"

"A hotel."

"Yeah, I figured that," she said. "It wasn't like I was expecting you to take me to your house even if your friend hadn't burned it down—"

"My friend didn't burn it down," he protested. Blaine felt bad enough over what had happened; he actually felt worse than Ash had over the loss. Except for some years growing up, he hadn't spent much time in that house. Few of his assignments, but for this one, had been in Chicago, so he'd stayed in other cities or woods or foreign countries.

Her lips curved into a slight smile. She hadn't missed his defensiveness with Reyes. But then he suspected that she didn't miss much. Her intelligence, in the form of her hacker skills, was legendary.

That was why he had assumed she was the one selling out national security. It was also why so many other people had assumed the same about her. He needed people to keep thinking that, but he didn't want to push her. He had already pushed her enough for one night.

The night was over now, though. The sky was light, the lake beyond the hotel glowing as the sun began to rise. She gestured toward it.

"But why did you bring me here?" she asked.

"Did you want to go back to the hotel where the speed dating took place?"

She shuddered—maybe as she envisioned that man he'd shot in the hallway outside her room. "No. But I didn't want to be this far away from the city, either. I have to work in the morning." She pushed open the passenger's door, stepped out and turned her face up to the sky.

Her skin glowed like the water, like the sky, and her beauty stole away his breath for just a moment. He had to stay behind the wheel of the SUV until he could catch it again.

She turned back to him. "It's already morning…"

"Almost," he agreed as he stepped out, closed his door and walked around to join her on the passenger's side.

She still held on to her door, holding it open. "We should head back to Chicago. I need to go to my apartment and get a change of clothes."

He could see the goose bumps raised on the pale skin of her arms and shoulders. He closed her door and clicked the locks of the SUV. Then he slid his arm around her slim shoulders to guide her away from the vehicle but also to warm her. Instead of settling against him, she tensed and held herself away from him. "This hotel has a boutique," he told her. "We can buy you some things here."

"But we need to go back to the city," she protested.

"We need to get some sleep," he said as he continued toward the lobby.

"I don't need sleep," she said. "I stay up all night a lot when I'm working. You probably do, too."

He had spent a lot of sleepless nights over the years. "But we don't know who is after you," he said. "We don't know who or how many." He had a grim idea, though. Anyone and everyone. "We're going to need some rest so that we're both alert to the danger you're in."

"Both?" she asked.

He nodded. "Of course."

She fell silent again, except for a few comments about trying to pay as they bought some things from the boutique and checked into a suite. It was just one bedroom, a bath and a sitting area with a pull-out bed. But it was clean and freshly painted with soft carpeting beneath his feet. She waited until he closed the door behind them before she spoke again.

Then she asked, "Why 'of course'?"

He shrugged. "You're in danger. So of course I'm going to protect you." It wasn't his usual job, though. But he'd protected himself well enough over the years that he figured he could protect her, too.

"But less than twenty-four hours ago you wanted to arrest me for treason and now you're going to protect me?" She shook her head. "I don't buy it."

"Buy what?" he asked. Did she think he really meant her harm? That he had no intention of keeping her safe?

"You don't want me to put out the word that I'm not selling that information," she said. "You're using me."

"How's that?" he asked.

He knew how he'd like to use her—since she was still wearing that damn sexy red dress. Something of what he was thinking—of what he was lusting—must have shown on his face because she slapped him.

Her palm just struck his shoulder, though, not his face. And maybe she'd only meant to shove him back since he'd stepped closer to her than he'd realized. Close enough to kiss her again.

He wanted to kiss her again.

"You want to dangle me as bait to draw out all these dangerous people," she said, the usual brightness of her green eyes dimmed with accusation and hurt.

The woman wasn't just brilliant at hacking. She was smart. Period. She could read people as well as she could read computers.

"I might not have worded it quite like that," he said.

But he couldn't deny it. She wasn't a threat to security, but he could use her to draw out other threats.

"But it's true," she said. She peered beyond him to the door he'd just closed as if she was considering running for it. Running from him. "You expect me to risk my life."

"No," he said. That was suddenly the last thing he wanted—her life at risk. "I will protect you. I won't put you in danger."

"You can't promise that something won't happen to me," she said. "You just said that you don't know who these people are or how many there are—or even how dangerous they are."

He nodded. "I don't know that. But I know *me*. And I know that I will protect you. Or die trying…"

She shuddered. "That's not exactly reassuring. I'd rather we both live."

"That's the plan."

"No, that's your hope," she corrected him. "*I* have a plan."

"Why am I afraid to hear this?" he wondered aloud.

"Because my plan is better than yours," she said. Her sass was back.

And he was intrigued by her sass more than her plan. He would listen to it, though, once he could focus on anything other than her mouth and all the bare skin that dress revealed. And in order to focus, he needed to kiss her again.

But before he could reach for her, she was stepping up to him, winding her arms around his neck and pressing her lips passionately to his.

Chapter Eight

He stood stiffly in Claire's embrace, his body tense and hard as she wound herself around him. Her lips moved over his, but he didn't kiss her back. He didn't touch her.

Claire's face heated with embarrassment, and her heart sank with disappointment. The earlier kiss had just been a ruse to protect her.

And she had just made a complete fool of herself.

She pulled away. But then he was touching her. One hand cupped the back of her head and held her mouth to his while his other hand was on her hip, pulling her tightly against him. He kissed her.

He kissed her like Claire had always wanted to be kissed. He kissed her with an intensity and passion that had her toes curling in her high heels. The hand on her head tangled in her hair while the hand on her hip squeezed.

Heat overwhelmed her—heat of passion, not embarrassment. She opened her mouth and invited him in, and he deepened the kiss. She wanted more than this, though. She wanted to strip off his sweater and vest, as she'd imagined earlier, and she wanted his naked skin sliding over hers—nothing separating them.

Even as she trembled with need, she summoned her strength and willpower and pulled free of him. She stumbled back a couple of steps—maybe because of the heels or maybe because her legs shook and threatened to fold beneath her.

"And here I thought I wasn't going to like your plan," he murmured.

So he liked kissing her?

He panted for breath, and his eyes had dilated so that only a thin circle of blue rimmed his pupils. Maybe he really liked kissing her.

"That was your plan, too," she said.

"To kiss you?" He shook his head. "That definitely wasn't part of my plan. I just had to improvise earlier tonight."

"And now?" she asked.

"You kissed me," he said.

She had started it. "We have to get used to kissing each other," she explained, "if you really intend to go undercover as my boyfriend."

He narrowed his eyes at her. "What are you talking about?"

"You told Martin that you're my boyfriend," she reminded him. "Isn't that your *cover*?"

"What does that have to do with kissing?"

"I admit it's been a while since I've dated," she said. "But I believe that boyfriends and girlfriends kiss. Has that changed since the last time I dated?"

A deep chuckle slipped through his lips—lips she could still taste on hers. "The last time you dated someone, you were all about the PDA?"

"PDA?" she repeated.

"Public display of affection," he translated for her.

At twenty-five she felt old and out of touch. Since she worked with younger people, she often felt that way, though. But Ash Stryker was at least a few years older than she was, maybe even several years older, and presumably uptight. She shouldn't feel old and out of touch around him.

"We don't have to kiss in public to prove that we're dating," he said.

Maybe not. But she had watched, usually enviously, couples so in love that they didn't even realize they weren't the only two people in the world. Apparently her mother had felt like that when she'd fallen for the man she'd met online since she had left her family so easily.

"You're right," she said. "We don't have to kiss in public." She didn't want to be anything like her mother.

He narrowed his eyes again. "You make it sound like we might have to kiss in private…"

"You've gone undercover before?"

He laughed again, shortly and cynically. "I've gone undercover a lot."

"Then don't you think we should get more comfortable with each other, so that we don't raise any suspicions?"

Martin had seemed suspicious probably because he knew she had no time for dating let alone a relationship. And she hadn't told him about her intentions to cut back on her work and make time. She hadn't wanted to worry him that his hours might be reduced.

"And what exactly do you mean by more comfortable?" he asked with his own suspicions in his bright blue eyes.

"Just kissing," she assured him in case he thought she meant more.

"So you want to kiss me?" he asked skeptically.

Hadn't he noticed that she had thoroughly enjoyed kissing him?

"Why?" he asked. "What are you up to?"

"You're using me," she reminded him. "Dangling me as bait for all your terrorists…"

He flinched—probably because she'd made him sound pretty callous.

"So, in return, you want to use *me*?" he asked. "For kissing?"

She nodded, and her face heated again with embarrassment when she admitted, "I need practice."

"What?"

"Like I said, I haven't dated in a while," she explained, "so I'm out of practice. I don't want to go out with my potential matches from the dating service and totally embarrass myself." Like she just had with him…

"You joined a dating service?" he asked.

She nodded. "Yes, that's how I wound up at the speed dating event. They sponsored it."

"You're really serious about meeting someone?" he asked as if the idea appalled him.

Now, with gunmen after her, might not be the best time to begin a relationship, though. "Yes," she replied.

"And you want to use me for practice?" he asked, but he didn't seem quite as appalled now.

"Yes," she said with a sigh of relief that he understood. "You can help me hone my dating skills."

"Why would you ask me for help?"

"I'm not asking," she pointed out. "If you want me to risk my life, I want something out of this. I will also help you figure out who really offered the information for sale. So you owe me."

He tilted his head as if considering her proposition. "You can figure out who?"

"I can hack the hacker," she offered. "I'll find the person while you use me to flush out the terrorists." She would have anyway, but he didn't need to know that.

"And you'll use me for dating tips?"

"Not tips," she said with a derisive snort. "I doubt you date any more than I do. I just want to use you for practice."

"Why me?"

"You'll be posing as my boyfriend anyway," she said. "And I won't get emotionally involved with you."

"You won't?"

"You're an FBI agent," she said. "You're not my type any more than I am yours." She held out her hand. "Do we have a deal?"

He looked down at her hand and studied it for a long moment before he reached for it. But when his hand closed around hers, he didn't shake. He pulled her forward into his arms. And he kissed her again.

He kissed her as thoroughly as he had before, using his lips and his tongue and all his considerable skill. Maybe she was wrong about how much he dated. Maybe he found more time for it than she thought…because he was a damn good kisser.

He literally stole her breath away. He had her pulse pounding and her skin tingling. But before she could completely lose her mind, he pulled back and turned away from her.

"You can have the bed," he told her as he flopped down on the couch. "We need to get at least a few hours of sleep. Then I'll drive you to your office so you can start looking for who really offered that information for sale."

Dumb with desire, Claire only managed a nod of agreement. Then she forced her legs to move, to carry her through the doorway to the bedroom. Her body, which was all tense and needy, didn't want to go to bed alone.

"Claire…"

His deep voice stopped her. But she didn't dare turn

back to him because she might ask for more than his kisses. She might join him on that couch and beg him to make love to her.

"Yes?" she asked and hoped he didn't hear how her voice cracked with desire.

"You really don't need any practice…"

IF THE WOMAN got any better at kissing she was going to be lethal—to his self-control and to his sleep. While he'd lain on the couch a few hours, he hadn't slept at all. His body had been too tense, too achy with desire. He'd been relieved when she'd come out of the bedroom, dressed in something other than that damn red dress, and told him she was ready to go to work.

He would have rather she'd said she was ready to go to bed—with him. But kissing was dangerous enough. He couldn't make love to her or he would be risking her life and his because he would be too distracted to protect her.

Hell, he was probably too distracted now.

While she worked at her desk, he'd taken a seat on the credenza behind her so he could watch her work. But he just watched her. She was so beautiful—her skin so flawless and such a pale ivory, her features so delicate and perfect. And her hair was such a bright, pale yellow. It kept sliding across her face and tangling in her lashes. She pushed that stray lock behind her ear but it kept escaping.

The next time it escaped, Ash pushed it back for her, skimming his fingertips across her silky cheek. Then he hooked that errant lock behind her delicate ear.

She shivered and looked up at him. "You're making it hard for me to work."

Did she feel it, too? Did the desire burning inside him burn inside her, too?

He cleared his throat before asking, "I am? So you haven't found anything?"

She shook her head, and her voice was sharp with frustration when she replied, "No. I haven't. But I don't work well with someone hovering over me."

"I could have told you that," her assistant murmured from the doorway of her office. He shot a resentful glare at Ash and asked, "Don't you have a job?"

"Martin!" Claire admonished him.

Ash shrugged off the kid's comment. "Of course. But it was more important to me to make sure that Claire is safe today after the break-in last night."

The kid's face flushed a deep red. "How are you going to keep her safe? Are you a cop?"

She'd been right when she had said that people might be suspicious of their sudden *relationship*. Her assistant obviously was. Or at least he was suspicious of Ash.

"I'm not a cop," Ash said. While some FBI agents had begun their careers in local law enforcement, he and Blaine had been recruited from military. So he wasn't lying until he added, "I'm just an overprotective boyfriend."

"But Claire's not in any danger," Martin said. Then he turned to her. "You're not, are you?"

"Of course not," she assured the kid. "Ash is just what he said—an overprotective boyfriend." She smiled at him with her lips, but her gaze was sharp with a warning he had already heeded.

He slid off the credenza, leaned over and pressed a kiss to her forehead. "I'll feel better once the police find out who broke in here last night and why."

"Probably for the bank stuff," Martin said. "Who wouldn't want access to bank accounts?" His face flushed—probably as he realized he had violated Nowak

Computer Consulting protocol. He wasn't supposed to talk about clients.

Was that how the auction had been traced back to Claire? Because of this kid running his mouth?

Resisting the sudden surge of anger at the thought of Martin putting her in danger, Ash instead agreed, "Who wouldn't?"

Getting into a bank account was what had gotten Claire in trouble. Though given the facts, he could understand why her hurt sixteen-year-old self had acted so rashly and resentfully.

Claire glared at him.

Martin uttered a nervous laugh. "Sorry, Claire, I forgot about—"

She waved a hand in dismissal. "It's okay."

"What are you working on?" he asked. Then he glanced at Ash again. "Or trying to work on?"

"Just checking my files," she said, "making sure nobody accessed anything."

She'd already known last night that no one had.

"Was anything accessed?" Martin nervously asked.

"No." But she touched the snow globe on her desk as if trying to assure herself that it was all right. That nothing had tarnished that memory with her father.

The assistant nodded. "Of course. Who would be able to get past your security?" He glanced at Ash again, as if wondering how he had.

Ash wasn't sure how he had gotten Claire to trust him. Actually he wasn't entirely sure that she did. But at least she'd agreed to work with him.

For a price.

Kissing practice.

That price might be more than he could afford to pay and still retain his sanity.

"Since you're done here, sweetheart, let me take you to dinner." They'd come in to the office late, so it was already close to six o'clock.

With a sigh she signed off her computer and nodded in agreement. "That sounds good."

"You're leaving already?" Martin asked, clearly as shocked as he'd been when Ash had claimed to be her boyfriend. "You never leave this early."

"I did yesterday."

"It's fortunate that you did," Ash said. "What if you'd been here when the office was broken in to?" He shuddered as if imagining the horror.

Claire must have imagined it as well because she shivered. A man had been shot; she could have been, too.

Except that she was worth more alive than dead— until she refused to offer up the information. Then she would die.

Ash couldn't let that happen. Maybe he had been a fool to use her as bait. What if he was already too distracted to protect her?

Claire grabbed up her big purse from the floor next to her desk. It was too big to fit into a drawer. "Let's go," she said. "I'm starving."

Or maybe she just wanted out of the place where a man had been shot. She dug in her purse while he and Martin cleared out of her office. Then she pulled out her keys and swiped a card from the chain through the automatic lock on the door. A red light flashed.

"You can go home, too," she informed Martin. "Last night was a late one."

"I came in late today like you did," he said. "I think I'll stay a little while longer."

Ash slid his arm around Claire's shoulders and escorted her toward the elevator. "Good night," he told the kid.

His reply was another glare from Martin. Of resentment? Jealousy?

Ash waited until the elevator doors closed to ask her, "Does the kid have a crush on you?"

She laughed. "Of course not. I'm pretty sure he thinks I'm ancient."

At twenty-five? Ash nearly laughed at the absurdity of anyone thinking that she was ancient. He doubted that Martin did, either. "If he's not jealous," he said, "then what's his problem?"

She shrugged. "I think he just doesn't trust you."

This hadn't been his smoothest undercover assignment. But still...

"Why not?"

"You showed up right after the building was broken into for the first time," she pointed out. "You don't think that looks suspicious?"

He sighed. "Damn suspicious."

She opened her mouth as if to say more, but he didn't trust security. So he kissed her.

Or maybe he kissed her just because he wanted to. He had wanted to since the moment she'd stepped out of the bedroom of the hotel suite. The red dress had been replaced with a long sweater and black leggings. But even with all that porcelain skin covered, she still looked sexy as hell.

He didn't stop kissing her until the elevator dinged and the doors slid open. Her thick lashes fluttered, and she stared up into his face, her green eyes dazed with confusion and maybe desire.

She didn't speak again until he helped her into the passenger's side of the SUV. Then she remarked, "I thought you weren't into PDA. You know there are cameras in the company elevators."

"That's why I kissed you," he said, although it wasn't entirely the truth. He had wanted to kiss her. "After the break-in, I don't have much confidence in your employer's security system. Anyone could be watching the footage from the security cameras."

She shivered despite her sweater. But then it was Chicago and the wind whipped through the streets, gaining in force as it pushed between all the tall buildings. But he suspected it wasn't the cold that chilled her. It was the danger.

"You think someone could have infiltrated our security staff?"

He shrugged. "Or maybe someone already on your staff was bought off. Like Martin…"

She shook her head. "Martin is just a kid."

He dressed like one, but Ash remembered Martin's employee record. He wasn't that much younger than Claire was. He was just immature. "Kids can make huge mistakes," he reminded her as he closed her door and hurried around to the driver's side.

His skin chilled now. It wasn't the cold; it was that sixth sense that told him someone was watching him. And it wasn't just his backup agents.

"You're never going to let me live that down," she groused as he joined her inside the SUV. "I made a huge mistake when I was a kid."

"You're not the only one," he said.

Her blond brows arched. "You did, too?"

He shrugged. "I wasn't necessarily talking about when I was young."

"You've made a huge mistake recently?"

He arched his brows back at her.

"Oh, about me," she said with a laugh. "You thought I was a criminal."

"It wasn't the only mistake I made," he said. As he started and steered the SUV out of her parking space, he peered around the lot. He recognized the vehicles of his backup units. But there were so many other vehicles in the lot.

"What other mistake did you make?" she asked.

He ignored her question for a few moments as he concentrated on traffic. Despite it still being during the rush hour, the streets weren't as congested as they should have been. That sense of foreboding rushed over him again.

"What mistake did you make?" she asked.

He pushed aside his concerns about being watched and replied, "I didn't think going undercover as your boyfriend would raise that much suspicion."

She emitted a self-deprecating laugh. "It probably wouldn't have if I was actually known to have a social life. But work has been my life for years."

Work had been his life, too. But he didn't harbor the regrets she obviously did. He didn't want more. He would never go speed dating for real.

"Sounds like work might be all I ever have," she murmured.

For him that was more a relief than a problem. "I should have known that I'm going to need to treat this assignment as I have all my other undercover assignments."

"How's that?" she asked.

"When I go undercover, I totally immerse myself in the role I'm playing," he said. "I make myself actually believe that I am who I'm pretending to be."

"So what does that mean?" she asked.

"I'm going to *be* your boyfriend," he said. "For real."

But as strange vehicles closed in on them, he wondered if he would have the chance. Or if his assignment was going to end sooner than he'd thought. Than he wanted…

Chapter Nine

Whatever Ash meant about being her boyfriend for real, he didn't look very happy about it. His handsome face was grim as he studied the road and the rearview mirror.

"Don't look so thrilled about it," she murmured resentfully. "It's not like I really want you to be my boyfriend, either."

"What?" he asked. Either he was distracted or he hadn't heard her at all.

"If you don't want this assignment," she said, "you can get a different agent assigned to protect me."

She had his attention then as he shot her a quick glance. "A different agent? What are you talking about?"

"What are *you* talking about?" she asked. "Being my boyfriend for real? I already told you that you're not my type."

"Why not?" he asked.

She wasn't sure he really wanted to know or if he was just humoring her with the question. It wasn't as if he was paying her much attention. His focus seemed to be completely on the roads, which she didn't understand since traffic seemed lighter than it usually was this time of day.

Not that she left the office this early all that often. But leaving later helped her miss the worst of the traffic jams.

"Why am I not your type?" he asked again. Maybe he really wanted to know.

"Because you're too uptight," she said. "That is totally not my type. I want someone laid-back, relaxed, funny…" That was what she had requested from the dating service for her potential matches.

"And you think another agent might be more your type?" A muscle twitched in his cheek as he tightly clenched his jaw. She could almost hear his teeth grinding.

No wonder he hadn't protested her calling him uptight. There was no doubt that he was.

"Maybe Agent Reyes," she suggested. "He's funny. Relaxed. Good-looking…"

"Maybe he would be more believable as your boyfriend," Ash readily agreed.

Hurt struck her like a stomach pang at how easily he would dump her—even as her fake boyfriend. She'd decided before, at the speed dating event, that maybe she wasn't ready for a relationship yet. Apparently she wasn't.

Maybe she was better off just focusing on her job. She hadn't made any progress on finding out who had posted that not-so-subtle auction of security information. But then she'd been distracted—because of Ash.

Maybe it would be better if he dumped her. For some reason she doubted that Special Agent Reyes would distract her as much as Ash did. While the other man was good-looking, he wasn't Ash Stryker.

"So you're going to hand this undercover assignment off to him?" she asked. *Just like that? Without an argument?*

He must have already been tired of dealing with her— of protecting her. Or maybe he really didn't like her stipulation on his using her as bait. Maybe he really didn't want to kiss her.

"I may not have a choice," he murmured.

Finally she realized why he had been so intent on studying the traffic as two big vehicles drew up close to them. One had crossed the yellow line to hem them in while another drove too close between them and the traffic parked alongside the street. It clipped vehicles, tearing off bumpers and crushing driver's sides. She gasped in shock and fear.

Then the vehicle on Ash's side moved closer, and metal rubbed against metal as they brushed. The passenger's window lowered and the gun protruded, the barrel nearly touching the glass of Ash's window.

She screamed as the gunman fired right at his head.

ASH FLINCHED EVEN as the shot glanced off the bullet-proof glass. Then he uttered a ragged sigh of relief that he had signed out the SUV equipped with all the latest and greatest in protection.

Claire stared at him in shock. "How did the glass not break? How are you not dead?"

"FBI SUV," he said. But not all of their vehicles were equipped like this one.

The gunman fired again and again, but none of his bullets penetrated the glass. So the driver edged the panel van closer, squeezing the SUV between it and the other panel van. The sides were plain white where usually a company logo would have been painted.

But then these guys weren't likely to advertise who they were working for.

Ash pressed hard on the accelerator. But another panel van had pulled in front of him.

"Hang on!" he warned Claire as he slammed his front

bumper into its rear bumper. Metal crumpled, and the van swerved—but not enough for him to pass it. Not with the vehicles alongside him.

He had already flipped on the two-way radio when that sense of foreboding warned him that something wasn't right. Chicago traffic was never this light. He'd been hoping the Bureau had blocked off streets. Now he understood it wasn't the Bureau at all.

It was whoever was after Claire. Another country? Home-grown terrorists? Or, as Reyes suspected, the Mob?

He touched the radio again—the radio that had been curiously quiet. Had his backup agents been taken out? That foreboding chilled him even more as he worried that was what might have happened, that the other FBI agents had been neutralized.

Murdered…

Claire probably wouldn't get her wish to work with Reyes then—even if Ash was gone. But then if Ash was gone, she would be, too.

"Where the hell is my backup?" he yelled at the radio.

But they couldn't reply to him—not if they were already gone. He couldn't imagine anyone getting the drop on Reyes, but for the information it was believed Claire had, the interested countries and groups would send their best. Maybe their best was better than Reyes.

Maybe their best was better than Ash…

"No need to shout," Reyes replied, his deep voice emanating from the speaker. "I haven't missed a thing."

Relief rushed over Ash, chased by a twinge of discomfort that Reyes had obviously overheard his and Claire's entire discussion.

The agent confirmed his suspicion when he said, "So, Ms. Molenski, you think I'm good-looking?"

She screamed in response as the panel vans closed in, pushing against the sides of the SUV. But the metal was reinforced and strong enough that it didn't crumple. "They're going to kill us!"

Apparently she didn't think the other agent was so funny now and that he was maybe a little too relaxed.

"They're not going to kill *you*," Reyes assured her.

No. Ash was the one who would die because he was the one standing in the way of these men fulfilling their mission, which was capturing Claire.

She glanced over at him, her green eyes bright with fear. Was she worried about him? Did she care?

"They will kill me," she said.

Disappointment flashed through him. She was worried about herself. But then again he couldn't blame her. It wasn't as if she even knew him since she actually thought he was uptight, and she had already wanted to replace him.

With Reyes...

The other agent said, "No, they won't. They need you alive."

"To torture me," she said.

Ash flinched—not because of the attack. Bullets continued to barrage against his window and the tires and sides of the vehicle. He flinched because he really shouldn't have told her about the torture. But he had needed her to agree to his protection—even though he wasn't doing a very damn good job of it.

"Then they'll kill me," she said, "because I'm not going to be able to give them the information they want."

Despite the vehicles pushing against his, Ash took one hand from the wheel and covered hers that was braced against the console between them.

"I will protect you," he promised. Then he snarled at the radio, "Get us the hell out of here, Reyes."

He accelerated, but he couldn't push the van in front of him out of the way. The back of the van began to crumple, though, the doors folding in.

"Take the next right," Reyes directed.

Ash slammed on the brakes and the vans, going faster, passed him, giving him room to do as Reyes directed.

"There's no road," Claire protested.

But Ash twisted the steering wheel anyway and the tires jumped the curb.

"This is a sidewalk," he told Reyes. It was actually a pedestrian walkway. He was just confirming—not questioning—the other agent's directions, though.

No one knew the city like Dalton Reyes. He had grown up on these streets. Ash had just been transplanted here in his adolescence when he'd come to live with his great-uncle after his parents had died.

Despite it being a pedestrian walkway, there were no people walking along it. When Ash had been worried that his backup had been neutralized, they had, instead, been busy clearing the area. Yet even without the people, the walkway was barely wide enough for the SUV to pass through without scraping the building or the fence on either side of it. A sign snapped as the bumper struck it. A press box crunched against the passenger fender.

Ash ignored it all and accelerated, trying to widen the distance between him and those vans. But at least one had turned onto the walkway behind him. Its grill grew larger as it bore down on them. Then it struck with such force that his and Claire's heads snapped forward.

"You okay?" he asked with concern.

Claire's shiny yellow hair was tangled over her face,

hiding her eyes. But he could feel her fear in the tension in her body. In the breath she held. Maybe it was because she was holding her breath that she didn't answer him and, hopefully, not because she was hurt.

The van bounced back off the reinforced rear bumper of the SUV, and then it swerved and crashed into the side of a building. Its tires had gone flat. Ash hadn't heard the shots, but he knew a sniper had taken out the tires.

His backup had been there all along, clearing the area and setting up snipers. But had they had enough time? Was the area completely cleared? Were there enough snipers?

He was driving the SUV up to another street, so he asked, "Which way?"

"Right again," Reyes advised.

Ash wrenched the wheel and made a right into oncoming traffic as he drove the wrong way on a one-way street. Cars sped straight toward them.

Claire's held breath escaped in a scream of terror.

A van also steered toward them—one of those panel vans—and it struck the SUV in a head-on collision. The fenders and hood crumpled on the van and the windshield shattered in a spidery web.

Another van was done. But at least one more was out there. Maybe more...

Ash slammed into Reverse. But the SUV bumper was caught, twisted and hung up on the mangled bumper of the crumpled van. He was stuck. Another van, also driving the wrong way, pulled up behind him. The doors slid open on the damaged van and gunmen jumped out. The barrels of their automatic weapons pointed at the SUV.

Ash wasn't sure how many bullets the glass could

withstand. How many could it take before it weakened and broke?

He pushed Claire's head down below the dash—just in case—as shots rang out.

Chapter Ten

Ash pressed hard on the accelerator and slammed the SUV into the already damaged van and into the gunmen. Then he jerked the SUV into Reverse, running over the men coming up behind them. He smashed the front of that van while dragging the other one along with him. Tires squealed and metal crumpled.

He twisted the wheel hard and spun the SUV around, which finally jerked the van loose from the front bumper. He sped off down the street—the right way. He didn't need Reyes's help anymore. Ash had lost Claire's would-be attackers. And as he headed back toward the hotel, he made sure he didn't pick up any new tails.

"Are you okay?" he asked her again, taking his attention briefly from the traffic to glance at her.

She nodded, but her face twisted into a slight grimace of pain.

"Your neck is okay?" he asked. "You didn't get whiplash?"

She nodded again—more easily this time. "I'm fine, thank you."

"How about you, Stryker?" Reyes asked, his voice emanating from the radio again. "You okay?"

"I'm alive," Ash replied, "so you're not taking over for me yet." And he clicked off the two-way radio. Not only didn't he need Reyes's help, he also didn't need his input during his conversation with Claire.

But there was no conversation. Claire was silent again the entire route to the hotel. Maybe she was afraid that more assailants would try to abduct her. Maybe she had another reason for her silence.

"Are you going to be disappointed about that?" he asked.

"About what?" she asked distractedly as she now nervously studied the street ahead and the street behind them. Her gaze darted around fearfully.

"That Agent Reyes won't be going undercover as your boyfriend," he said.

She turned toward him with a furrowed brow, as though she was totally confused.

"I thought that's what you wanted," he said. He could have listed her reasons why—because the other agent was relaxed and funny and good-looking. Obviously she didn't think Ash was any of those things.

"I thought that's what *you* wanted," she said. "You don't seem really thrilled about this assignment."

"I'm not thrilled," he admitted, "when someone's trying to kill me."

She uttered a short laugh. "Then why in the world are you an FBI agent?"

He had his reasons, but he had never voiced them aloud. Only the people who knew him well had figured out why. But very few people knew him well. Now he fell silent.

They didn't speak again until he locked the door to the hotel suite behind them. Then she turned on him, standing close as if she could intimidate the truth out of him. All she made him do was want to kiss her.

And more…

"You know why I became a hacker," she said. "Isn't it only fair that you tell me why you're an agent?"

"The Bureau recruited me out of the marines," he said.

She stepped closer and narrowed her gaze. "You're doing that thing you do."

"What thing do I do?"

"That thing where you tell the truth but it's not really the truth." She shook her head as if she'd confused herself. "But it's not a lie, either. It's just not the entire truth. You're leaving something out."

Uneasiness lifted the hair on the nape of his neck. He was nearly as on edge as he'd been when he had realized something wasn't right about the traffic. But now he was uneasy because Claire had already gotten to know him better than most people did since she'd figured out his trick.

"The Bureau recruited me," he said. "That's the story of how I became an agent."

"But I didn't ask you how," she reminded him. "I asked you why. Sure, the FBI recruited you, but why did you say yes? It wasn't like my situation where I had no choice. Either I did my job or I did time."

Since she had only been sixteen when she'd committed her crime, her time probably would have just been served in a juvenile detention center, and she would have had her life back sooner. Instead she'd made hacking her life.

Her green eyes widened in shock. "Or is that why you said yes? Because you didn't have a choice?"

"I had a choice," he said. And he'd chosen what he'd always wanted to do. He just hadn't realized how easy it would be for him to achieve his almost lifelong goal.

She sighed in resignation. "You're not going to tell why, are you?"

He shrugged. "There's nothing to tell. Some little boys

dream of growing up to become firemen or policemen or astronauts."

"And you dreamed of growing up to become an FBI agent?" she asked skeptically.

"Yes."

She tilted her head and studied his face. She had more questions. He saw them in her gaze. But before she could ask anything else, her phone rang from the depths of her bottomless purse. By the time she found the cell, the phone had stopped ringing.

"Who was it?" he asked the questions now.

Her brow furrowed as she studied the screen of her phone. "I don't recognize the number."

His pulse quickened. What if it was a buyer? "We need to get a trace on your phone."

"But that online post doesn't give out a phone number," she reminded him. "The exchange details are to be worked out once the bidding is closed."

"But since I'm not the only one who traced that post back to you—"

"Incorrectly," she interrupted.

"Incorrectly," he repeated to placate her and because he felt bad over his accusations. "Someone might try to make contact with you—"

"Without accosting me in a parking lot?" Her phone trilled again. "I have a voice mail." She punched in some numbers and played the message on speaker.

"Claire, it's Leslie. I know you're busy and you turn down my every request for you to come to dinner, but you need to take a break every now and then and come up for air. And food. Please give me a call back. I'd love to catch up with you."

"I bet he would," Ash murmured.

Somehow her old mentor must have heard about the

break-in at his former employer. He had contacts inside the company yet. Maybe a mole…

If he were truly retired, why was Leslie Morrison still so interested in Nowak Computer Consulting?

"Call him back," Ash told her. "And accept his invitation."

Her eyes widened in shock. "People are trying to kidnap me and you want me to go to dinner at a friend's?"

"Not alone," he said. "You'll be bringing your boyfriend along, of course."

"If we can't fool Martin, we'll never fool Leslie," she warned him. "In fact, Leslie may be extending this invitation just to check you out…if he heard about you. He still has friends at the company." Her brow furrowed again. "So he could be calling about the break-in, too."

Ash was pretty sure that he was calling about the break-in—maybe wanting to know how much Claire knew about it and maybe about the online auction, too. Ash had only agreed that the man wasn't a suspect in order to placate Claire. To him, everyone was a suspect—but her.

"Leslie will believe I'm your boyfriend," he assured her.

"Why?" she asked. "Because you're going to make yourself believe it?"

He'd told her how he immersed himself in his undercover assignments. "Yes."

She laughed. "I don't think you know how to be a boyfriend."

He couldn't argue the point. He couldn't remember the last time that he had been anyone's boyfriend. He'd dated but never for long. A relationship wouldn't have survived his being gone for months on end for undercover assignments, so he had never even tried.

"You're more a bodyguard than a boyfriend," she said.

He flinched at the description. He didn't do protection duty. He did *undercover.*

"Isn't a good boyfriend protective?" he asked. "Doesn't he make sure his girlfriend is safe?"

She laughed again and shrugged. "Since, as an adult, I haven't had a real boyfriend, I wouldn't know."

"Well, you're about to find out," he said. He stepped closer, tempted to show her with his lips and his hands. Instead he clasped her hand around her phone. "Call Leslie Morrison back and accept his invitation to dinner for you and your guest."

"We won't fool him," she warned even as she began to dial the phone.

"We will."

Her lips curved into a half smile. "Because you think you can fool yourself into believing you're my boyfriend."

Ash was worried that he was fooling himself—because this assignment was unlike any other he ever had. Except that it was probably even more dangerous…

THE FOLLOWING DAY Claire had called in sick to work—something she had never done before. Of course that had been mostly because she hadn't dared violate her probation. But even though she hadn't been at work, she had been working—on the laptop with the backup hard drive she'd pulled from her voluminous purse. She always carried a lot of hardware and software with her.

She turned toward Ash and glared at him. "You should have let me keep working," she said. But she wasn't sure if she was irritated that he'd made her stop to come to Leslie's dinner party or if she was irritated with how sexy the man looked in black slacks and a blue

sweater that matched his eyes and was loose enough to
hide his weapon.

"Were you making any progress?" he asked.

No. She'd been too distracted while confined in that
small hotel suite with him. She'd been too distracted with
thoughts of his kisses and concerns that he hadn't kissed
her again. Why hadn't he kissed her again?

He leaned closer to her, as if he was considering it now
as they stood on Leslie's front porch, the doorbell they'd
pushed echoing softly inside the craftsman-style house.

But then Leslie's nine-light front door finally opened.
"Claire!" he greeted her with delight. "You're more beautiful than I remember."

Her face heated with embarrassment that she had been
caught dressing up. From the hotel boutique she'd bought
a shimmery green dress that she'd thought flattering.
But she'd gotten more of a reaction from Leslie than she
had Ash. He kissed the air near her cheek, then turned
to her date.

"Speaking of beautiful," her former mentor murmured.

Claire fought back a laugh at Ash's reaction. Of course
it was minimal—just a faint widening of his blue eyes.
But she loved that he'd been caught off guard by Leslie's flirting. At over six feet with a bald head, her former
mentor often caught people off guard with his orientation.

"I'm Leslie Morrison."

"Ash Stryker." He held out his hand.

Leslie clasped it in both of his. "I'm so happy to meet
you."

"Thank you for inviting us to dinner," Ash said.

"I've been trying to get this one to come over since I
retired," he said. "But she kept saying she was too busy.

Now I know why…" He winked. "Dinner is almost ready. Fortunately for you I cooked instead of Ed."

"It smells wonderful," Claire said as she followed Leslie inside the warm and colorful home.

Ash leaned forward and pressed his lips to her neck. "You smell wonderful," he whispered.

She shivered in reaction to his closeness and to his warm breath on her bare skin. So now he was going to play the part of her boyfriend…?

"Ah, I remember being that in love," Leslie murmured wistfully.

Another man stood in the dining room, cradling a baby in his arms. Like Leslie, he was also burly but sensitive. His voice soft with hurt, he asked, "You're not in love anymore?"

Leslie slid his arm around the man and the baby. "I'm more in love with you, with our family, our home than I ever thought possible."

Her old mentor had everything he wanted; Leslie Morrison posed no threat to national security. Claire had never doubted him. And now she had no doubts about what she wanted in life.

She wanted the loving partner, the children, the home…although hers wouldn't be nearly as clean and decorative as Leslie's. And her food might be take-out instead of the wonderful Cornish hens and stuffing he'd served.

"You're quiet," Ash mused as they left Leslie and Ed waving after them from their front porch. "Are you upset?"

She was unsettled but mostly from the way he'd acted in front of Leslie and Ed. Loving…

He had always had a hand on her. Either on her hand or her leg or, like now, her back, as he escorted her to the parked SUV. He had immersed himself so completely in the role of her boyfriend that she wasn't sure if he believed it, but *she* was beginning to believe that he was actually her boyfriend.

Or maybe she only wished that he was. But if he was, she would never have the life that Leslie had. She would never have the children and the house; she would never really have him because the FBI would always come first. He would go undercover somewhere else—with someone else—and maybe he would so totally immerse himself in that cover that he would forget all about her.

No. She had been right when she'd told him he wasn't her type. The sooner they found the real hacker and she was no longer in danger, the sooner she could get back to her search for someone who actually was her type, for someone who wanted the same things she wanted out of life.

Who wanted a life…

"Are you upset?" he asked again as he helped her into the passenger's side of the SUV.

She waited until Ash slid behind the steering wheel before she replied, "This was a waste of time tonight."

He flashed her a grin. "Isn't this what couples do?" he asked. "Hang out with other couples?"

"You didn't make me accept that dinner invitation so we could socialize," she said. "You wanted to investigate my former mentor."

She had seen some of what he'd been working on today since they'd both been on computers in the living area of the suite. He had accessed all Leslie's financials; of course he would have had FBI clearance to hack, especially with national security at risk. He had also slipped away for an extended visit to the bathroom during dinner, and she was pretty sure that he'd managed to search the house.

He didn't deny his motivation. He didn't say anything at all as he concentrated on traffic on the drive toward their hotel.

Remembering the other time he had been so focused on traffic, she shivered with fear. She glanced around, too, but she noticed nothing out of the ordinary. But then she hadn't last time, either, until it had nearly been too late.

"I investigated him," he finally admitted.

"Then you must have found out what I already knew. Leslie is no longer a hacker." He was a happily retired man who was enjoying his family.

Leslie had Ed. Her dad had Pam. Claire had nobody but an FBI agent who was using her as bait to draw out terrorists. She needed this to be over soon.

"We should have stayed in the suite," she said, "so I could have kept working on finding the real hacker."

"Have you made any progress on that?" he asked.

She shook her head, frustrated about that and maybe frustrated over how Ash had kept touching her throughout dinner. Without his touch she felt cold. Maybe she should have brought along a jacket. But they were nearly back to the hotel now. She glimpsed the lights ahead.

"I can't find who posted that information sale," she said. "But I really don't believe that someone could bypass firewalls that I've made sure were secure."

He pulled the SUV into the hotel lot and parked it. Then he turned toward her. "Maybe there's a better hacker out there than you are."

The air whooshed out of her lungs as if he'd punched her stomach. "A better hacker?"

He chuckled softly at her reaction and opened the driver's door.

She thrusted open her door before Ash could walk around to the passenger's side. "Maybe there's a better FBI agent than you."

He reached beneath his sweater and drew his gun from his holster. "Maybe there is," he readily agreed. "But lucky for you I'm pretty damn good."

"What—"

She had no time to utter her question as he pushed her down to the asphalt. Then he fired so closely that the gunshots reverberated in her ears.

Light flashed in the darkness as Ash's gunfire was returned. Someone was out there shooting at them. She hadn't seen them, but Ash had.

How many were there?

If it was like the other day, with all those vans filled with all those armed men, she didn't like her and Ash's chances to survive.

He was a good agent, but was he good enough to save them this time?

Chapter Eleven

Ash had fired those first shots as warning shots. He didn't want to kill this time. He counted the shots fired back at him, all from one gun. He hoped like hell that that meant only one shooter.

"Stay down," he ordered Claire as he eased his weight off her.

"Where are you going?" she asked, panic in her voice.

"You'll be fine," he assured her. "There's only one of them."

And he couldn't let that one get away.

She grasped his arm, though, holding him back. "One of them can still kill you."

He chuckled again. "Not me..."

He was a better agent than she obviously thought he was. He wouldn't have lived as long as he had if he wasn't.

"Stay down," he told her again. Then, just as the last shot flashed in the darkness, he ran. And before the shooter could load another clip, he tackled him.

An elbow dug into his ribs; a fist grazed his jaw. He dodged the blows and pinned the man's limbs to his sides, subduing him.

"Who are you?" he demanded to know.

The man replied in another language. But he didn't offer his name. Instead, he called Ash a few. Fortunately for him, Ash was fluent in many languages.

Ignoring the insults hurled at him, he asked in the man's native tongue, "Who sent you?"

He couldn't just assume that it was the country the man was from. He suspected it was someone from the same country Ash was from—America.

"Did Leslie Morrison hire you?" he asked—again in the man's language although the shooter was apparently pretending he didn't understand since he didn't reply.

The guy had begun following them from Claire's former mentor's house. He had been waiting outside for them, so someone must have tipped him off that they would be there. Leslie was the only other person who knew they were coming to dinner. Unless he'd told someone else...

The guy cursed again but admitted nothing. He only struggled harder in Ash's grip and nearly broke free—especially when Ash heard the scream.

Claire screamed, her voice high-pitched with fear.

Maybe this man shooting at them had only been a diversion so that someone else could grab Claire. And Ash had fallen for the diversion.

And lost Claire.

CLAIRE'S THROAT BURNED from her scream. And her face burned from embarrassment when she turned toward the man she'd thought was grabbing her from the pavement to abduct her.

"You're okay," Agent Reyes soothed her. "I'm sorry for scaring you. You're okay." Then he called out more loudly, "She's okay."

She wasn't okay. She was terrified. And not just for herself. She was terrified for Ash, especially when she'd heard men speaking in some foreign language.

He had thought he only had one gunman to overpower. What if there had been more waiting for him?

She waited for him to call back, to assure them that he was fine. She heard a grunt, as if someone had taken a blow.

"Help him," she urged Reyes. "Make sure he's okay!"

Reyes laughed. "He's Special Agent Ash Stryker. Of course he's okay. The man is a legend."

Ash was older than her but not more than a decade—not old enough to have become a legend. Most people usually didn't become legends until after they were dead. She wanted Ash alive and well.

"Why do you say that?" she asked.

"As a marine, he survived his deployments to the most dangerous places in the world. As an agent, he's survived going undercover and arresting the most dangerous people in the world." He pitched his voice lower, and for once the grin left his face as he was totally serious and respectful, "That's why he's a legend."

She shivered with fear for all that Ash had survived. What if he hadn't survived?

Not only wouldn't she have met him but she also might not have survived the recent attempts on her life. When she'd said that he might not be the best FBI agent, she had been acting out of spite and wounded pride. She'd been wrong.

Ash stepped out of the darkness as suddenly as he had disappeared into it. But this time he dragged a man behind him.

Reyes groaned. "You killed another one. We can't question dead men."

"He's not dead," Ash informed him. "He's only unconscious."

The grunt must have been his because she could see no wounds on Ash. He hadn't been shot as she'd feared. And he hadn't been overpowered. Maybe he couldn't be overpowered if he was as legendary as Reyes thought him to be.

"He's all yours," Ash said as he thrust the man's limp body toward Reyes.

"You don't want to question him?" the other agent asked in astonishment.

"I already did."

"What did he say?"

Ash spoke in another language as easily as if it were his native tongue.

"What the hell does that mean?" Reyes asked.

"You don't want to know," Ash replied. "Let's just say it was more about my character than his. He wouldn't admit to who hired him."

"But you think you know," Reyes said.

"He was waiting for us outside Morrison's house."

"You can't think Leslie hired him," she said. Not after Leslie had showed them how happy and content he was with his family. "That man must have followed us there."

Reyes chuckled and then teased him, "You didn't notice a tail? Are you getting distracted like your friend Blaine got distracted?"

Wasn't that how Ash's house had burned down? Because Blaine had been distracted.

"No," Ash replied. "And you damn well know it."

Reyes shook his head. "I know it. But I don't understand how you're not." He gestured at Claire. "With her looking like that all the time."

After being knocked to the ground, she probably looked a mess with her dress all wrinkled and her hair all mussed up. But Ash hadn't been distracted even before he'd knocked her to the ground. He'd been aware of the tail—aware of the shooter in the parking lot before the man had even fired his first shot. No wonder Special Agent Ash Stryker was a legend—or maybe he just wasn't attracted to her—at least not enough for her to distract him.

Ash didn't look at her, but stared at the other agent through narrowed eyes. "Did you see a tail?"

"No," Reyes confirmed. "I was the only one following you."

She hadn't seen him. It was a good thing that she was a hacker instead of an FBI agent. "Are you sure he didn't follow *you*, then?"

The grin left Reyes's face again while Ash laughed. "He's relaxed," he said, "but not relaxed enough to let someone tail him."

"Leslie has nothing to do with this man," she insisted. She refused to believe that her former mentor's life wasn't as complete as it had looked. He couldn't want more— he couldn't want so much money that he would risk his freedom and his family to get it.

Reyes looked at Ash as if seeking his opinion. Ash just shrugged. Reyes made a gesture, and other agents materialized out of the darkness and carted off the unconscious man. "I guess we'll find out."

Ash shook his head. "I doubt you're going to learn anything from him. We need to bring Morrison in for questioning."

"You're going to interrogate Leslie?" she asked, completely appalled that he could eat food the man had spent the day preparing and then treat him like a criminal.

"Not me," Ash said. "I can't blow my cover."

She uttered a soft snort in derision. "Like anyone is really buying your cover."

"I'm not sure this guy would've taken him on if he'd known who he is," Reyes defended the agent whom he obviously idolized. "Or what he is, anyway."

"I'm not sure knowing I'm an FBI agent would have prevented any of these abduction attempts," Ash admitted.

"Then what's the point of this cover?" Claire asked. "You don't have to act like my boyfriend. You could just be my bodyguard."

Reyes whistled between his teeth. "Ash Stryker doesn't do protection duty."

"And this isn't," Ash said. "If everyone believes I'm just your boyfriend, there will be more attempts to abduct you."

Panic clutched her heart and she murmured, "Oh, lovely."

"There will also be a better chance that whoever really offered the information for auction will slip up and reveal himself," Ash added.

He was using her. She'd already known it. But hearing that reinforced her need to protect herself from him. She had to remember that he was only acting as her boyfriend. But the only thing he really wanted from her was to stop the threat to national security.

She shivered.

"You should take her inside," Reyes advised. "She's cold."

"And tired," Claire added. "I'm going to the suite."

"You can't," Ash said. "This place has been compromised. We don't know who he might have told where we are. We can't stay here."

"Good," she said.

She wasn't sure she could handle another night in a hotel suite with Ash Stryker—not after he'd acted so convincingly like her boyfriend earlier that evening. Her skin still tingled from all his touches.

But he wasn't her boyfriend; he was a legendary FBI agent, one who was never distracted or unfocused. She should have been grateful that he was as good an agent as he was, but her pride hurt that she didn't affect him like he affected her.

"I want to go home."

She wanted the comfort of familiarity—of her messy apartment and her lumpy mattress. "Please take me home."

"THIS IS NOT my home," Claire said, glaring at him as he carried her bag and her laptop into the hotel suite. "I wanted you to take me home."

"This is," he said.

She shook her head. "No, it's not. This is not my place."

He chuckled. "That's a good thing. It's not a mess like yours."

She shot him another glare. "Very funny. Is that why you brought me to another hotel—for the housekeeping?"

"Housekeeping is just a bonus," he replied. "This is my home."

She glanced around again and finally noticed that the suite was more lived-in looking than the one where they'd stayed the past few nights. He had more clothes here— some books. The suite also had a kitchenette and boxes of food sat atop the small counter.

"You've been staying here since your house burned down?" she asked.

"Yes," he said. "Whenever I'm in Chicago."

She walked around the room again as if taking an inventory of everything in the suite. "Is this all you managed to save from your house?"

He shook his head. "I wasn't able to salvage anything from the fire."

She sucked in a breath as if horrified. "You lost everything?"

"It's not like I had a lot to lose," he assured her. "I've always traveled light." He had been doing that for a long time.

"But you must have lost your pictures—your mementos—of your parents then." The glare was gone, her green eyes warm with sympathy as she stared up at him. "I'm sorry…"

"I didn't have any pictures or mementos of my parents to lose," he told her.

She sucked in another breath—now she probably was horrified of him, not for him. "You don't have anything to remember them?"

"They died in a fire," he explained.

Tears welled in her eyes. "That's horrible. I am so sorry." And then she was holding him, her arms winding around his back as she offered him comfort.

He waited for the questions. People always asked questions when he admitted that his parents were dead. They wanted details, wanted his emotions.

Claire asked no questions. She only offered comfort. But then she had a great relationship with at least one of her parents, so she must have been imagining how upset she would have been if she'd lost her father.

He didn't want her sympathy because he didn't deserve

it. His hands on her shoulders, he eased her away from him. "It wasn't like that."

"Like what?" she asked. "Two people died, leaving you without a father or a mother. That must have been horrible."

"They weren't good parents," he confessed. "They weren't good *people*. They—and a lot of innocent people—died in a fire they started with bombs."

She gasped. "Your parents set a bomb?"

"Yeah," he said.

"You were there?" she asked, her voice shaking as if it was happening now, as if he was in danger all over again.

He nodded. "But, obviously, I was rescued before it went off."

"That's good…" She breathed a sigh of relief. "How old were you?"

"Eleven," he said. "Old enough to know what they were planning was wrong. I called the FBI." Actually he'd called his grandmother, and although she had already passed away, her brother had answered his cry for help. Uncle George had been an FBI agent. "They got there in time to get me out and some other people, but not everybody…"

"I'm sorry," she said. "No matter what else they were, they were your parents. It was a loss for you."

He shrugged off her sympathy again. "The parents of a special agent with the FBI's antiterrorism division were homegrown terrorists—talk about irony, huh?"

"It's not ironic at all," she said. "It makes perfect sense. Now I understand why you became an agent." And she hugged him again, her arms winding tightly around him. "I'm so sorry."

He tried to ease her away again because her sympathy

was affecting him. His heart was warming and aching with longing—with affection. With...

He jerked away from her. "So it's not exactly home, but I think you'll be comfortable here."

"Are you?" she asked as she looked around again. "It's not exactly homey."

His home hadn't been homey, either. Uncle George had been a bachelor his whole life, a man who'd traveled so much that he'd never spent much time at home until he'd inherited guardianship of an orphaned child. He had retired from the Bureau—many years after he could have—to take care of Ash.

"Are you having your house rebuilt?" she wondered.

He shrugged. "I'm not sure I need a house. If I hadn't inherited it from my uncle, I wouldn't have given up my apartment. But the real estate market had bottomed out then, so it wouldn't have been a good time to sell."

"Your uncle passed away, too?" she asked with another gasp of shock and sympathy.

"He was my great-uncle," he explained. "He lived a long life."

"But it must've—"

Hoping to erase that look of sympathy from her beautiful face, Ash goaded her. "He was a bachelor. That was probably why he lived so long."

And the glare was back, directed right at him. "I know what you're doing," she said. "You're trying to make me mad at you so I'll stop feeling sorry for you."

"That's because there's no reason for you to feel sorry for me," he told her.

"There is a reason," she stubbornly persisted. "You just don't like that I feel sorry for you. That's why you're trying to push me away."

"True," he conceded. "But do you know what I do

like?" Instead of pushing her away, he pulled her into his arms—tightly.

She shook her head.

"Kissing you…" And he lowered his mouth to hers. He had started kissing her to get that aggravating look of sympathy from her face. It was gone now…as he lifted his head slightly. And it was replaced instead with the flushed, excited look of passion.

Now he worried that he wouldn't be able to stop kissing her.

Chapter Twelve

During one of his deployments Ash had been embedded. He'd been unable to move, barely able to breathe. But he had survived. He wasn't certain he could survive being embedded with Claire Molenski—not when he would much rather be in bed with her.

But that would be a mistake. And that was why he'd stopped himself from kissing her those few nights ago. He couldn't afford to be distracted and he knew that making love with her would distract him. He doubted he would be able to get her out of his mind and then he might miss the next tail, the next gun pointing at him out of the darkness.

He had to be careful with her safety. And with his heart.

She was getting to him with her quick wit, with her impressive intelligence and with her heartfelt sympathy. Not to mention with her soft touch and her silky lips…

Right now her hair was clipped on top of her head. She wore fleece pajama bottoms and a hooded sweatshirt. But she still looked sexy as hell to him. She didn't even look at him. Instead, she studied her laptop screen, her face tense with dread and betrayal.

He knew why. It wasn't because she was still searching, but because she had realized what he had before the speed dating event. He was the one to offer his sympathy now. "I'm sorry…"

"You already knew," she said with a sigh.

"I don't know who," he said. "Just that someone at your company is behind the information auction." The access being offered for sale was for clients of only Nowak Computer Consulting, so only an employee of Nowak would know who all those clients were.

"You thought it was me."

He nodded.

"I don't blame you," she said with another sigh. "I would think it's me, too."

"You would rather think it's you," he said. After all the time he'd spent with her, he was beginning to know her character well. "You don't want to believe that someone you work with would betray your company and your country."

She sighed. "No, I don't."

"It could have been someone that you once worked with that still has access."

"Leslie?"

She didn't sound as certain of his innocence as she'd been before. But now he wasn't as certain of Morrison's guilt, either. "He was interrogated."

"And?"

He shrugged. "We can neither confirm nor deny whether or not Leslie Morrison is a suspect."

She snorted. "Sometimes you're such a suit."

He wasn't wearing one now. Like her he had opted for casual, but jeans and a button-down shirt were as casual as he got while on the job. Unless he was undercover…

"If we're going to confirm or deny," he said, "I need to get in a suit again. I need to do some investigating of my own."

Instead of relying on someone else to interrogate a suspect, he needed to be doing the interrogating himself. But if he'd interrogated Morrison, he would have blown his cover.

Her shoulders and back straightening, she tensed. "Are you handing me off to another agent?"

He tensed, too, at the thought of trusting her protection to someone else. "No." But he didn't like what he was about to suggest, either. "We've already established that we're getting nowhere in this hotel room."

Except closer to the bedroom. He wanted her so badly. He had to get out of there.

She smiled. "So we're getting out of here? Are we going to the office?"

"I can't keep you safe there," he said.

"Why not?" she asked. "I need to get back to work."

He pointed at her laptop. "You've been working nonstop. Yours isn't the kind of job where you have to go into the office every day."

"But I can't stay away indefinitely," she said. "I need to go back."

"Not yet," he said.

"When?" she anxiously asked.

"Not until this is over. I already raised suspicion spending that one day in the office with you," he reminded her. "I can't justify my presence and maintain my cover as your boyfriend."

"Not without looking like an overprotective control freak." She tilted her head and stared at him in consideration. "Are you?"

He chuckled. "Only when you're nearly kidnapped every time you step outside…"

Resigned to not going to work, she frowned. "Then I can't step outside."

"We have to," he said, maybe a little more forcefully than necessary since her eyes widened with surprise at his harsh tone. "We're not going to find out who's behind the auction unless we flush out his buyers and hopefully him, too."

She tensed again. "So I'm back to being bait."

"Yes," he said but he was reluctant to use her again, reluctant to put her in danger. He would make sure he had an excellent team watching them—a team that wouldn't let any would-be abductor anywhere near her.

"Okay," she agreed with less reluctance than he felt. "If it gets me out of here, I don't even care." She jumped off the couch and headed for the bedroom. But she caught the jamb and turned back. "Where are we going?"

"Movie..." But that would make it difficult for his team to see would-be abductors in a dark theater. He shook his head. "No. Dancing..."

"I don't dance."

He brought up their earlier bargain. "You wanted to practice dating on me," he reminded her. "Dancing is part of dating."

"Not for everyone."

"What if it is for someone you want to date?" he asked.

She rolled her eyes. "I doubt that it will be. The service I joined makes sure to make only compatible matches. So why would they match me with someone who loves to dance when I don't?"

"How do you know you won't love it, too?" he asked. "Unless you try."

She groaned. "But if I love it, I'll have to change my dating profile."

He mocked her groan. "Then you'll get more potential matches..."

She smiled. "Good point. I will have more potential matches. You'll teach me?"

"I'll teach you." He would teach her how to dance with another man. Regret and jealousy twisted his stomach muscles. It wasn't what he wanted.

He wanted her.

CLAIRE HAD AGREED to act as bait just to get out of the close confines of that hotel suite. She'd been going crazy with wanting Ash. But dancing with him was worse. He was too close, his body touching hers, his hands on her...

"Sorry," she murmured as she stepped on his foot again. "I don't remember the last time I danced."

"There wasn't dancing at your dad's wedding?"

Warmth flooded her along with the happy memories. "Yes, but I only danced once—with my dad."

His hand tightened on her hip as he steered her into a turn around another couple on the floor. The other couple was older, probably in their seventies, but they moved much more gracefully than she did.

Ash had brought her downtown to a piano bar that played more slow songs than she was comfortable dancing to. She would like to blame her inability to dance on being so uncomfortable in his arms. But she felt more than discomfort. She felt attraction—more than she'd ever felt for anyone else.

He leaned down, his mouth nearly brushing her ear, and asked, "Were all of the male guests blind?"

She shivered at his warm breath caressing her ear. He must have thought she was cold because he pulled her closer.

"There weren't a lot of single men there," she said. "The rest were relatives or married or both."

She had barely paid any mind to any of the men there,

though. She hadn't noticed anything but her father's happiness. It was only later as she'd wished him and Pam a long and wonderful marriage that she'd realized she wanted that happiness for herself.

She wouldn't find that with Ash Stryker no matter how she wished that she could. His closeness and his touch affected her, making her ache and long for more. But he had nothing to give her—emotionally.

But maybe she could get something from him physically—like dance lessons. The skill would lead to more potential matches.

"So teach me how to dance," she said.

He steered her around another couple. "You think I know?"

"You told me that you would teach me," she reminded him of their bargain. "And you must know how since you're not stepping on my feet."

The pianist began another song, singing along in a smoky voice, "I could have danced all night..."

Ash bent her back over his arm in a dip so dramatic that her hair nearly brushed the floor. "Maybe I know a move or two," he murmured.

A giggle slipped out of her lips, but she held back another one. She had given him such a hard time about being uptight that she couldn't admit now that he was actually fun. He kept showing her moves—twirling her around so that she felt light-headed and giddy.

And happy.

Ash Stryker made her happy. He seemed happy, too, the grin still on his handsome face. She stared up at him, wanting to rise up on tiptoe and kiss him. She could have explained that she was only playing the part of his girlfriend. But she didn't trust herself to only kiss him—not when she wanted more.

Then he dipped her again, over his arm, and then swung her back up so that her face touched his. Cheek to cheek, breaths mingling. Maybe it was just from the exertion, but she imagined that her panting echoed his. They were both struggling for deep breaths; their hearts beating hard in their chests nearly in as perfect unison as their steps now were.

She wanted to kiss him—deeply. But the music stopped. The other couples applauded the pianist, who was apparently going on break for the first time since she and Ash had arrived. They sprang apart now, awkwardly.

"Would you like a drink?" he asked.

Since she couldn't have what she really wanted, she nodded. "I am thirsty."

They hadn't left the dance floor since they'd arrived. So they had no table and had to push their way through the crowd to the bar.

But Ash, with his naturally commanding nature, summoned the bartender immediately. He handed her a wineglass while keeping a glass of water for himself. That glass of water reminded her of what she'd wanted to forget—that he was on duty. He was only doing his job.

"How do you know what kind of wine I drink?" she asked as she sipped the tart white.

"I saw a wine bottle in your apartment," he said. "I believe it was near the front door."

"I intended to recycle it," she explained, then laughed at his skeptical look. "I do recycle."

"Hopefully your potential match will, too."

"And dance…" She was surprised by how much she enjoyed it. Or was that only because she had been dancing with Ash?

"You can add it to your dating profile," he said. "You're a fast learner."

"How do you know how to dance so well?" she asked. "Did you learn in the marines or the Bureau?"

He chuckled as he led her away from the bar. "I had two left feet at the Marine Ball."

"So the Bureau…?"

He nodded. "Undercover assignment."

"I thought you went undercover among dangerous people," she said as she followed him through the crowd. At least that was what his groupie Reyes had told her.

"Didn't you watch *Black Swan*?"

"You were in a ballet?"

He laughed so hard that his blue eyes twinkled and crinkled at the corners and deep creases formed in his handsome face. Her breath caught with awe at his masculine beauty. And she stumbled again, this time over her own feet.

"No," he said, and the grin slid off his face, replaced by a look of wistfulness. "But I had to get close to a dancer to get some information."

Her chest hurt, maybe over her held breath. Or maybe the pang she felt was of jealousy. She suspected that dancer had been female and beautiful and that Ash had gone undercover as her boyfriend, too.

Had that poor woman known who he really was?

Or had she thought it was real?

At least Claire knew the truth. Ash might have tried to convince himself his cover was real. But Claire couldn't fool herself. She had done that once before when she'd convinced herself she was doing the right thing by hacking into her mother's lover's bank account and giving away all his money. That had cost her her freedom for a number of years. Fooling herself over Ash would cost her her heart.

Maybe forever…

The music began to play again.

"That was a short break," she murmured regretfully. She wasn't sure that she could dance with Ash again. Being that close to him, moving that intimately with him...

Ash reached for her wineglass—probably to put it onto a table and take her back into his arms. But when his hands were busy, another man grabbed her elbow.

"Dance with me," he implored her.

He was tall and dark and handsome. But not as tall or dark or handsome as Ash.

"She's with me," Ash said.

"It's just a dance," the man told him with a brow raised as if he thought Ash was overly possessive. She glared at the FBI special agent, warning him not to blow his cover with an overreaction. Despite what Ash believed, not everybody was trying to abduct her.

"It's just a dance," she assured Ash. But when she'd danced with him, it hadn't been just a dance.

But then the man swept her onto the dance floor, and she realized it was much more than a dance—when she felt the gun barrel digging into her ribs.

"You will not scream, Ms. Molenski," he warned her. "You will not betray any hint of fear or panic."

She wasn't an FBI special agent. When she was afraid, she damn well showed it. She wasn't a robot like this man appeared to be. "I—I can't..."

He moved like Ash had, swinging her around other couples on the dance floor, taking her farther and farther from where Ash stood between the dance floor and the bar. And with every spin, the gun barrel dug more deeply into her ribs.

She needed to scream. But would Ash hear her above

the music? Would he know she was in trouble before the man pulled the trigger?

Before she could catch Ash's gaze, the man spun her entirely off the dance floor. Then he nearly dragged her down a short hallway that led to a back door. He released her to grab the handle of that door.

And she turned to run.

"Come with me," he said. "Or I will shoot."

She was tired of being afraid. She was tired of this man and his empty threats. Rallying her courage, she pointed out, "You can't kill me and get the information you want."

"I'm not going to shoot you," he said. "I am going to go back inside and shoot your boyfriend."

Hoping he was bluffing again, she shook her head. "You can't go back in that crowded bar and just shoot him."

"Watch me," he challenged her. And with his weapon drawn he turned back toward the dance floor.

While she hadn't identified any of them, there were other agents in the bar offering backup protection. But she wasn't sure who they were or if they were really even there. But she'd seen Ash in action before; he might not need backup to defend himself.

But what if an innocent bystander got struck in the cross fire?

She would never forgive herself. "Wait!" she called to the man. "I'll go with you."

She told herself it was because of the danger he posed to everyone else, but she knew the only person she was really worried about was Ash.

Until the man opened that back door and dragged her out into a dark alley…

Now she was worried about herself. She had chosen not to run or scream in order to protect Ash.

Now who would protect her?

Chapter Thirteen

Ash's wounded pride had cost him valuable time. If her wanting to dance with the attractive stranger hadn't made him jealous, maybe he would have reacted faster. Maybe he would have grabbed the guy before he had pulled Claire away from him onto the dance floor.

Just before the guy had walked away out of view with Claire, Ash had noticed the bulge beneath his jacket. The man was armed. And he wasn't another agent. He was a threat.

He was a danger to Claire.

Ash hurried onto the dance floor. But couples crowded the area and the man had kept twirling Claire faster and faster until they disappeared from sight.

Where the hell had he taken her?

The piano bar wasn't that big. That was one of the reasons that Ash had chosen it for their dance date. Probably the other reason was that the pianist played mostly slow, romantic songs. As much as he'd wanted to get out of the close confines of the hotel suite, he had still wanted that closeness with Claire—without the risk of his losing control of his desires.

He had lost control, though, because he hadn't been thinking clearly—his brain clouded with his attraction to her. And now he'd lost her.

He tapped the listening device in his ear and turned on the two-way radio. He hadn't activated it earlier because he hadn't wanted Reyes or any other agent's voice in his head. He'd been having enough issues ignoring his own voice whispering how beautiful and smart Claire was—how desirable.

He also hadn't wanted Reyes or any other agent overhearing his conversation with Claire because he was never sure what he might tell her. He had already shared more with her—about his past, about his life—than he had anyone else. Very few people knew about his parents. But he had told her.

She hadn't judged him as others had based on what his parents had been. That was why, as he'd gotten older, he'd learned to share his past with only the people he trusted. He trusted Claire. Not at first but she had earned his trust with her honesty, her integrity, her caring about others. And when he'd told her about his parents, she had understood and accepted him in a way no one else ever had.

Then he had used her as bait again to flush out threats to national security. Guilt and regret hit him like fists in the stomach. Sure, he had promised he would protect her; he'd even believed that he would keep her safe. But he'd failed her.

"Where is she?" he asked aloud, drawing the curious glances of some of the dancers.

"We lost eyes on her," a voice replied in his ear.

But the woman of one of the dancing couples leaned away from her husband and touched Ash's arm, drawing his attention. He had noticed them earlier, though. While in their seventies, they moved lithely, with grace and a harmony that had come from years of dancing together. Her voice soft with concern, the older woman told him, "Your wife went out the back with that man."

Her husband groaned and tried to spin her away. "Edith, don't get involved—"

Edith dug in her heels, refusing to follow her husband's lead this time, and said, "But she looked so scared. She didn't want to leave with that man."

The woman understood the brevity of the situation, but the man just shook his head, obviously thinking that she was overreacting.

She wasn't.

"You shouldn't have let her dance with another man," Edith's husband advised him. "That's a sure way to lose your woman."

Edith slapped his shoulder. "And acting like a possessive caveman is another way to lose her…"

Ash was already walking away but he heard the older man's comment as he headed off the dance floor. "I've kept you fifty years…"

The older woman giggled as youthfully and giddily as Claire had earlier when Ash had dipped her. He shouldn't have let her dance with another man.

But she wasn't his wife. She was, however, his responsibility. Maybe he shouldn't have taken responsibility for her. Protection duty wasn't his specialty. Sure, he'd always survived his undercover assignments. But he had always gone undercover alone, not even with another agent whose safety he'd had to worry about, let alone a civilian. She was smart and savvy, but she wasn't a trained agent.

"She's out back somewhere," he told the others through the two-way radio. "We need to find her before he gets her in a vehicle."

Or she would be forever lost to him.

THE ALLEY WAS so dark that Claire wasn't even sure where they were anymore. No streetlamps illuminated the narrow space between tall buildings. There weren't even lights burning by back entrances to whatever businesses the buildings housed.

She stumbled, and the man nearly lost his grip on her arm. So she did it again in a desperate attempt to wrestle free of him.

His hand tightened around her arm, painfully squeezing. "Knock it off," he warned her. "You're not getting away from me."

"It's the heels," she said. "I'm not used to wearing them." That much was true. She had learned from Ash how to go undercover. But she wasn't pretending to be someone else, as he often did. This man evidently knew exactly who she was, and that was why he'd grabbed her.

"You looked pretty damn graceful dancing with your boyfriend," the man said.

She had felt graceful dancing with Ash. His lessons had made her graceful because she had never had any grace before. She'd been born a klutz; that was why the snow globe her father had given her depicted her riding on his shoulders instead of trying to skate herself. While the day had been perfect, she hadn't been able to learn to skate as easily as Ash had taught her to dance.

"I'm not graceful," she insisted. "It was all him."

"You were smart to leave with me," the man said. "Your boyfriend will live to dance again."

She was both relieved and regretful. Ash would be so mad that she hadn't called out for help, that she hadn't drawn his attention. But then he would have been shot for certain.

"What do you want with me?" she asked as she stumbled again.

He jerked her arm. "I want nothing from you. I am only doing my job."

Not only did he look like Ash, but he had the same philosophy. He was only doing his job. She nearly laughed, but she was too close to hysteria to risk it. She needed to keep her wits about her. She wasn't graceful, but she'd always been smart.

"Your job is to kidnap me?" she asked. She needed to get him talking. She needed to distract him somehow so that she could get away from him.

"My job is to bring you to my employer," he replied.

Maybe he didn't consider it kidnapping because he wasn't going to ask for a monetary ransom, but she did. And the ransom they wanted was information she couldn't give them.

"Who is your employer?" she said.

"You'll know soon enough," he answered.

Thinking of the torture Ash had warned her about, she fearfully asked, "What does he want with me?"

"You'll know soon enough," he repeated as he jerked her arm again, trying to pull her along as he quickened his stride.

She stumbled again, this time for real. Her ankle twisted, and she fell. Asphalt bit into her shins, and she cried out at the pain.

The man swung toward her with his gun, pointing the barrel at her head. "Stop playing games."

"I'm not playing," she insisted.

"Your whole online auction wasn't a game?" he asked. "You ask for bids but reply to none of the offers?"

She'd been keeping track of the action, too, and had noticed that the seller hadn't accepted any offers. It was almost as if he'd changed his mind. Or maybe he'd realized the FBI was on to him. While Ash may have convinced himself he was her boyfriend, nobody else had bought his act...except maybe for her.

"What makes you think I'm the one selling information?" Claire asked the question she had asked Ash what seemed like so long ago. But it had only been days—days since he'd suspected her of being a traitor to her country.

"What?" the man asked. "Have you changed your mind? Is that why you replied to no offers?"

Cognizant of how close the gun was to her face, she gingerly shook her head. "I am not the one who offered that information for sale," she said. "I would never betray my country."

"Not even for a good price?" he asked.

"Not for any price. The risk is too great," she said. "Not just to the economy and the governments of several countries but personally, too. Giving up that information would cost me my freedom."

"Not giving it up will cost you your life," the man threatened, and he cocked his gun. "Now get up!"

If his employer wanted information from her, he was unlikely to kill her. But he still might shoot her. Like torture, a gunshot wound wasn't something she wanted to experience. So she struggled to her feet, but when she tried to put weight on the ankle she had wrenched, she fell again.

"Stop playing!" he yelled.

"I think I sprained my ankle," she said. Maybe. Or maybe she'd just broken the heel on her shoe. But she wasn't going to admit to that. Maybe if he thought she couldn't walk, he would just leave her in the alley.

Instead, he moved the direction of the barrel of his gun. "Get the hell up!" he yelled, his impatience—what little he possessed—gone. "Or I will shoot your damn leg."

She called him on what she hoped was a bluff and asked, "Then how will I walk wherever you're taking me?"

"I don't know how you will," he said. "But you will or I'll shoot your other leg, too."

"You don't want to do that," a familiar male voice spoke from the darkness.

Conflicting emotions overwhelmed Claire. She was relieved for herself that Ash had found her but also terrified for him. The stranger's gun was already cocked and ready to fire.

"You don't want to get involved," the man advised him.

"I am already involved."

"You're the boyfriend…" The man sighed. "Well, Ms. Molenski, looks like I'll be breaking that promise I made you." He fired before she could even scream a warning to Ash.

It was dark in the alley. The man wouldn't have been able to see Ash well. He had to be okay. And she had assurance that he was when he leaped over her and knocked the man to the ground.

Grunts and groans echoed off the walls of the brick buildings as the two men grappled in the alley. She scooted back as feet kicked out near her and a fist swung.

And a gun barrel…

"Get down!" Ash ordered her as another shot rang out.

She was already down. But she laid flat on the asphalt as more bullets and pieces of cement and mortar ricocheted off those brick walls. Shots echoed all around her as if coming from hidden stereo speakers on full volume. She wasn't sure who was shooting now. The man or Ash.

Ash had to be wearing a bulletproof vest like he'd worn one before. He had to be safe as he struggled to protect her. Why was he struggling alone?

Where was his backup?

Then she realized that the echo of shots wasn't coming just from those fired in the alley. There were shots being fired beyond the alley—out on the street.

Like Ash hadn't come alone to protect her, the stranger hadn't come alone to kidnap her. Their backup was also in a shoot-out.

If the other agents didn't prevail, Ash might have more than this one man to fight. Even as great a special agent as he was, he wouldn't be able to fight them all—not if there were as many as it sounded like there were.

It sounded like a war raged outside the alley. And another one within it.

The men continued to struggle over the firing gun. But then the clip must have emptied out, as the shooting stopped inside the alley. And then moments later the struggle stopped.

The shooting outside the alley also stopped, and an eerie silence fell. All Claire could hear now was her own heartbeat thudding heavily and quickly in her ears.

"Ash…" she called out softly.

But there was no reply from either man. So she rose to a crouch. Ignoring the pain of her already scraped legs sliding over the asphalt, she crawled over toward where the two shadows lay in the alley.

"Ash…" she called out again. "Are you okay?"

Still no reply.

She was close now, right next to those lifeless bodies. She reached out, only to put her hand on the ground, but instead of touching asphalt, her fingers sank into something warm and sticky. A pool of blood.

Chapter Fourteen

Ash struggled to regain consciousness; he had to protect Claire. Had this man's backup gotten into the alley while he was struggling with her abductor? Had one of them grabbed her?

He'd chosen to go alone into the alley and have his backup concentrate on the ends of the alley to make sure that no one could escape with Claire. Maybe he'd made the wrong choice.

He cleared his throat and called out her name. "Claire…"

"I'm here," she said. "I'm right here." And her hand touched his face. But it was wet.

"Are you bleeding?" he asked her.

"No. I think you are."

He shook his head. "No. It must be him…"

The man had stopped struggling. Ash hadn't wanted to kill him; a dead man couldn't tell him who'd hired him. And he was obviously a hired gun working for someone else. But he hadn't been working alone.

"We need to get out of here," he said. "Have you really hurt your ankle?"

"I think I just broke the heel on my shoe," she said. "I can move. Can you?"

He was still lying on the ground. The other man had

fought hard and fired so many damn shots that Ash was struggling yet to regain his breath.

"You're wearing your vest, right?" she asked, her voice cracking with concern.

"Yeah, of course…" But now that the numbness was beginning to wear off, he felt the pain. The sharp, stinging pain.

She uttered a sigh of relief.

"This guy had friends," he warned her. "You might not be safe yet."

"What? You doubted me?" Reyes asked. His voice wasn't in Ash's ear but in the alley as the other agent joined them. "I've been handling stupid thugs like that my whole life."

"You took care of them all?" Ash asked.

"A couple of the guys are on their way to the hospital," Reyes replied.

He heard the sirens now and saw the glint of flashing lights at the end of the alley.

"I don't know if they'll make it," Reyes admitted. "What about this guy?"

The guy in question grunted and moved slightly as he began to regain consciousness. He wasn't dead.

Ash should have been relieved that they would be able to question him. But he felt a pang of regret. Or maybe it was just of pain. He grimaced.

"You are hurt," Claire said, her tone accusatory over his lie but also concerned.

"I'm wearing a vest," he reminded her. But the bullets had been ricocheting off the brick walls. It was why he'd told Claire to get as low as she could. Had one of those bullets struck him somewhere the vest didn't protect?

He had recently almost lost his best friend, Blaine, when the special agent had been shot in the neck. He had nearly bled out and would have if Ash and Reyes hadn't been there. Ash moved his hand across the ground beside him; blood had pooled beneath him.

Reyes dropped to the asphalt next to him. "I think you've been hit, Ash." He touched his two-way and demanded, "Get some medics back in the alley immediately. Stryker's got a GSW."

Claire gasped. "Are you in pain?"

He hadn't been at first. He must have been in shock. But now pain radiated throughout his body, so much so that he wasn't entirely sure where he'd been hit. He tried to move, but Claire pushed him back to the ground.

"Stay still," she said. "Wait for the paramedics." Her voice rising with panic, she shrieked at Reyes, "Tell them to hurry."

He must have looked bad. She sounded more scared for him than she had sounded for herself when she'd thought she was alone in the alley with her kidnapper. From the shadows, he had listened to her talking to her abductor.

But she'd been smart. She had bought him time to get to her. Of course she'd been smart; she was a brilliant woman. And beautiful…

He wanted to tell her that, wanted to tell her how much he admired her spunk and her spirit. But footsteps pounded against the asphalt as paramedics and more agents ran down the alley to them.

Two of the paramedics dropped to the ground next to him while another paramedic and an agent turned their attention to the man Ash had injured.

A male medic flashed a light in his face and shone it over his body. "Sir, can you tell me where you've been shot?"

"I'm fine," he replied because he wasn't entirely sure. "A bullet must have just grazed me."

"You're bleeding, sir," the other paramedic said. "We need to know where it's coming from but we can't see here." They began to lift him onto a stretcher they'd carried into the alley.

"I can't go anywhere," Ash protested. He had to question the suspect even though the man wasn't fully conscious. Ash had slammed the guy's head against the asphalt until he'd dropped the gun. But it wasn't the man about whom he was really worried.

"You have to go to the hospital," Claire told him.

He gripped the sides of the stretcher, trying to lift himself off it, but he still hadn't regained his strength. "No, I can't."

"You have to," she insisted, rising up with the stretcher as the paramedics raised it. She swayed unsteadily on her feet. "They have to check you out."

"I have to protect you," he said. She'd said it was just a broken shoe heel, but he suspected she was really hurt.

"I'll do that," Reyes offered.

"I want to go with him," Claire insisted. "I can ride in the ambulance, too."

"She should ride along," Ash agreed, mostly because he didn't want to let her out of his sight again. "She should get her ankle checked." But the stretcher and the paramedics kept rolling him away. And he wasn't sure how effectively he could protect her in his present condition.

Reyes waved at him and called out, "We'll meet you at the hospital."

Ash respected Reyes as a special agent. He would trust the man with his life, but he wasn't sure he could trust anyone with Claire's life. He had nearly lost her himself; he didn't want to take any more chances with Claire.

He shouldn't have used her to lure out more buyers. He should have focused on finding the hacker who'd offered the information for sale. But that person had to be someone Claire worked with—someone she knew, someone who might also pose a threat to her life.

He finally regained his strength enough to sit up on the stretcher. But it was too late. The paramedics had lifted him into the back of the ambulance and closed the doors.

He had to trust that Reyes would protect Claire. He had to trust that he would see her again.

CLAIRE SLIPPED QUIETLY past Reyes, whose attention was on the tall blond man with whom he spoke just inside the double doors of the emergency room. Fortunately the ER doctor had exchanged her broken heels for a pair of slippers, after he'd wrapped her sprained ankle, so that she could move quietly. She didn't move painlessly, though, since every step had her flinching.

But she had to see Ash. She had to make certain that he was really okay. There had been so much blood in the alley. Some of it was still on her hand, staining her skin. She shuddered as she glanced down at it.

Reyes had assured her that Ash was invincible; that no stray bullet was going to keep him down. Sure, he'd lost a lot of blood. But the bullet wasn't even in him; it had gone through his thigh and just nicked an artery.

Nicked?

She had scoffed at the agent obviously trying to downplay a serious injury. Ash could have bled out in that alley. He could have died trying to save her.

That was why she'd left with the stranger—to protect him. But Ash had been so determined to protect her that it had nearly cost him his life. And still, even as they'd been wheeling his stretcher away, he had been worried about her safety. She had to see him, to make sure he was really okay and to show him that she was.

So she had convinced a sympathetic nurse to give her Ash's room number. After hobbling across the ER, she boarded an elevator to the tenth floor. Her painkillers must have worn off because her ankle throbbed. But she ignored the discomfort and hurried down the corridor to his room.

She could hear the deep rumble of his voice even before she pushed open the door to his room. And she breathed a sigh of relief that he sounded good, strong. Happy even…

Then she saw why he sounded so happy. He cradled a bald-headed baby in his arms while a woman with curly dark hair adjusted the pillows behind his back. Then the woman leaned over and kissed Ash's cheek before dropping a kiss on the baby's forehead.

"You really are an angel," he told her with an appreciative smile.

"I love you, too, Ash," the woman said and kissed his cheek once more.

Pain struck Claire again, but it wasn't her ankle that was throbbing now. It was her heart that hurt, clenching in her chest. She'd thought Special Agent Ash Stryker was all about his career but maybe that had just been part of his cover posing as her boyfriend.

Maybe he was really a family man with a wife and a baby. She gasped as that pain overwhelmed her, and she whirled away from the doorway to duck back into the hall before anyone saw her. But as she whirled around, she slammed into a wall of muscle so hard that she bounced off and nearly fell.

Strong hands gripped her shoulders, holding her upright. "Easy," a man's deep voice murmured.

She glanced up into eyes that were a crisp green with a gaze so intense she was certain that the man missed nothing. He was blond and broad and vaguely familiar. She realized he was the man to whom Reyes had been talking when she sneaked past him. Apparently she had only sneaked past Reyes, not him.

"Are you all right?" he asked her.

She nodded, but the pain gripping her heart hadn't lessened its hold. She flinched, which probably betrayed how she was feeling.

"The doctor said your ankle is sprained," he said. "You're supposed to stay off it, Claire."

"You know my name?" she asked. After what had happened at the piano bar, she should have known better than to trust anyone. But there was something about this man, a protectiveness that inspired trust.

"Yes, I know who you are," he said. Taking his right hand off her shoulder, he pulled a badge from beneath the neck of his shirt. "I'm Special Agent Blaine Campbell."

"Oh." So this was Ash's good friend…

She wanted to talk to this man, wanted to ask him questions, but laughter drifting from the hospital room distracted her. Who was that woman?

She hadn't asked her question aloud, but Blaine replied anyway. "That's my wife and baby in there with Ash."

The laughter grew louder, and irritation replaced her pain. She retorted, "No wonder you burned down his house."

"You've been talking to Reyes," he remarked. Even though amusement glinted in his eyes, Blaine Campbell uttered a weary-sounding sigh.

Since she hadn't actually talked that much to the man, she clarified, "I've been listening to him."

"I wouldn't recommend that," Blaine said with a sharp jerk forward as Reyes pushed him from behind.

"Hey, don't go bad-mouthing me to Ms. Molenski," the dark-haired agent said.

Blaine snorted. "*I* would never do that. Too bad you can't say the same."

"Technically Reyes was bad-mouthing you to Ash," she clarified again.

Blaine snorted again. "Ash and I go back too far for that to get you anywhere, Reyes."

The other man nodded. "Yeah, if you burning down his house didn't hurt your friendship, I guess nothing will."

"Why would you want to hurt their friendship?" she asked Reyes. Not that she believed he really wanted to, he just enjoyed teasing people, especially those he considered friends, like Ash and Agent Campbell. It was clear that he thought as much of Blaine as he did Ash.

"Because he wishes Ash was his best friend," Blaine said. "Ash was the best man at my wedding."

Claire lifted her head, listening to the laughter coming from inside Ash's room. Blaine had really had the man currently flirting with his wife stand up beside him at their wedding?

"That's because he saved your life," Reyes said. "But he didn't do that alone. I was there, too."

Blaine grunted as if just the memory of his close scrape caused him pain. "You were there that time. But Ash saved my life many more times than that during our deployments."

They had both been marines, then.

"Honey," a woman's soft voice called out as she joined them in the hall. She must have overheard them. She touched her husband's arm. She had told Ash she loved him, but that love was clearly in her warm brown eyes as she gazed up at Blaine's handsome face. "You have to talk to Ash. He was already trying to get dressed to leave, so I handed him the baby."

"He didn't freak?" Blaine asked in astonishment. "Ash would be more comfortable holding a grenade."

The woman laughed. "That's what I thought when I saw the look on his face."

He had looked pretty comfortable to Claire. But she didn't know how long he'd been holding the infant. Apparently too long because he called out from the hospital room, "Hey…" His tone was soft and stilted, as if he was gritting his teeth and trying to keep his voice low, probably so he wouldn't frighten the baby. "Someone needs to get back in here."

"You all want to go down to the cafeteria for coffee?" Reyes asked.

"We should leave him alone," Blaine agreed.

Mrs. Campbell shook her head. "Not with Drew. He'll try to take him along wherever he's so determined to go."

"To Ms. Molenski," Reyes replied.

"Ms. Molenski?" the woman asked.

"Meet Claire Molenski," her husband introduced them. "Claire, this is my wife, Maggie."

The woman reached out for her hand, taking it in both of hers. "You're Claire. He was asking about you. He's anxious to see you."

The woman spoke with no jealousy or judgment. Clearly her love for Ash was like a sister's for her brother.

"Hey!" he called out again.

"He's anxious all right," Claire agreed. "Because you left him alone with your baby."

Maggie squeezed her hand. "He really is anxious to see you, to make sure you're all right. He cares about you."

Warmth flooded Claire's heart. But she refused to let hope burgeon. Ash cared about his assignment, about flushing out more bad guys and finding the hacker. He didn't really care about her. He wasn't a potential match.

"Come on," Ash persisted from inside the room. "I didn't volunteer to babysit."

"Let's go inside," Maggie urged, but it was Claire she pressed through the doorway first.

She forced a smile and teased him. "I thought you liked babysitting. Isn't that what you've been doing with me?"

"You've been on protection duty?" Blaine asked in surprise. "You hate that. You've always hated that." He flinched as his wife's elbow struck his ribs. "But I could be wrong."

"You are," Ash said. "I'm not on protection duty. I'm undercover." He carefully held out baby Drew to his mother. "I'm posing as Claire's boyfriend while we flush out the security threats."

"Well, that's way different, then," Blaine said with a grin. "She's in danger, and you're protecting her. That's not protection duty at all."

Ash glared at him. "Why'd you come along? Afraid your wife was going to leave you for me?"

Blaine laughed, obviously confident in his wife's love and loyalty. And Claire was suddenly jealous of Maggie Campbell again, jealous that the woman had the relationship Claire wanted for herself. Maybe it was that jealousy that overwhelmed her or maybe it was just exhaustion and pain, but she swayed on her feet as dizziness overwhelmed her.

"She's falling!" Ash cried out. But his warning came too late.

She was going down, and she was unconscious before she knew if she'd been caught or if she'd hit the floor.

Chapter Fifteen

Ash had failed Claire again. First he'd let the gunman get her on and off the dance floor. And then he hadn't caught her when she'd fainted. He'd tried getting out of bed, but his injured leg had folded beneath him and he had fallen.

Fortunately Reyes had caught Claire. Then he'd carried her back to the emergency room. He'd carried her away from Ash. Maggie, with her usual concern for everyone else, had hurried after them to make sure that Claire was all right.

Ash had wanted to go to the ER, too. But Blaine had helped him back into bed instead and assured him, "Maggie will let us know how she is."

"Why would she have passed out?" Ash asked. "Was she grazed with a bullet in the alley, too?"

"She just sprained her ankle," Blaine said. "But she shouldn't have been walking on it without crutches. The pain probably got to her."

"Why?"

"She's not a marine or an agent," Blaine said. "She's not used to withstanding pain."

"No," Ash said. "I mean why did she walk without crutches? Why didn't she stay in bed and rest?"

Blaine laughed.

"What?" He glared at his friend's amusement. "What's so damn funny?"

"For such a smart, observant guy, you're being pretty oblivious," Blaine said.

He still had no idea what his friend was talking about, but now he just shrugged.

And Blaine laughed again. "You really don't get it?" Then his smile slid away, and sadness darkened his eyes. "I forget that you're not used to it."

"Used to what?" Ash asked, wondering what had made his friend sad. Since he'd married Maggie, he'd been pretty disgustingly happy.

But Blaine didn't seem sad for himself. He seemed sad for Ash. He replied, "You're not used to people caring about you."

Blaine was one of the few people who knew Ash's parents hadn't given a damn about him. They would have blown him up with all those other innocent people if an FBI agent—if Uncle George—hadn't rescued him just in the nick of time.

"You think Claire Molenski cares about me?" He laughed now, knowing how much he infuriated the woman. "I accused her of treason. I've used her as bait to lure out potential terrorists. She hates my guts."

And he couldn't blame her. Had someone treated him the way he had treated her, he wouldn't have cared for the person, either. He would have resented and hated him, but his heart clenched with pain at the thought of her hating him.

"Sure," Blaine said as if humoring him. "That's why she put herself through pain to get up here to see you, to make sure that you were all right, because she hates your guts."

Could she actually care about him? Refusing to even

hope it was true, he shook his head in denial. "She probably was just telling me that she was going home."

To her apartment. To her life.

"It's too dangerous," Blaine protested.

"Of course it is," Ash said. "But that's my fault."

Blaine shook his head. "You're not the one putting her in danger."

"Yes, I am," he said as guilt overwhelmed him. "I could have let her post online that there is no way around the government firewalls, that she'd made certain there wasn't. But then I wouldn't be able to catch everyone willing to buy the information that would get them around those firewalls."

"So that's how you're using her as bait to flush out would-be terrorists?" Blaine sounded appalled.

But then he was the quintessential knight in shining armor. He always had to play hero to every damsel in distress.

Ash was the one who'd put this particular damsel in distress. But Claire had proven she wasn't helpless. She was smart, and she was strong. Or so he'd thought until she'd nearly collapsed onto the floor of his hospital room. Everyone had his or her limit. Claire must have reached hers.

"It was a mistake," Ash admitted.

Blaine sighed. "I understand what you were trying to do. You're always looking for the greater good. Sacrifice one life to save many…"

It was something Ash had had to do as a marine and as a special agent in the antiterrorism division. But he couldn't do it now, not when that one life was Claire's.

"It was a mistake," he repeated.

"You had a solid plan," Blaine said. "You were protecting her."

Panic flashed through him again as he remembered how quickly and easily he had nearly lost her. "I didn't do a very damn good job."

"She's not the one with a bullet hole in her leg," Blaine said.

"Reyes would claim that I got distracted."

Blaine snorted. "Like me?"

Ash couldn't deny that Claire distracted and captivated him. "Reyes likes talking smack."

"Are you sure that acting like her boyfriend is just a cover for you?" Blaine asked.

Ash nodded. "Of course. I made contact with her at a speed dating event. The cover as her boyfriend makes the most sense. It was the most believable." Even to him.

When he'd danced with her at the romantic little piano bar, he had felt like a man dancing with his girlfriend. Or as poor Edith had misinterpreted, his wife. She hadn't been wrong about Claire being scared and in danger, though. Once the shooting had begun, her husband must have realized that she hadn't overreacted at all. And that he hadn't reacted enough.

"I know how you go undercover," Blaine said. They had been assigned to different divisions over their careers, but occasionally they had worked together. And they had known each other too long.

Ash sighed in resignation; he couldn't deny whatever his friend was about to say.

Blaine continued, "You're all in."

He couldn't deny that was how he went undercover.

"So don't go thinking it's real," Blaine advised him, "unless…"

He wasn't sure he wanted to hear this, but he respected Blaine and respected his opinion. So he asked, "Unless?"

"Unless you want it to be."

Ash's heart slammed against his ribs as it began to pound fast and furiously. He forced a laugh, albeit a nervous one. He was calmer when people were shooting at him than being put on the spot about his feelings. He laughed harder. "Don't be ridiculous."

"I'm serious," Blaine said. "I saw your face when she collapsed. You care about her."

He couldn't deny that. "She's my responsibility. I'm the one who put her in danger. So of course I want to make sure she's all right."

Blaine narrowed his eyes as if considering whether Ash was speaking the truth or lying.

Maybe he was lying. To himself…

"I'm not like you," Ash insisted. "I'm not meant to be anyone's husband or, God forbid, father."

"I used to think that, too."

"But we all knew you were wrong about it," Ash said. "We all knew you would be a family man someday. You're too much of the protector. You need someone to protect—a wife, a child. I don't need anyone."

Blaine expressed his doubt with an arched brow.

"I don't need anyone," Ash repeated. "I never have and I never will." Maybe if he kept telling himself that, he would believe it.

CLAIRE HAD LEARNED her lesson about eavesdropping. While Reyes had been helping Maggie extricate herself from a group of nurses oohing over the baby, Claire had rolled her wheelchair down the hall to Ash's room. She had heard the end of his conversation with his friend.

And when Blaine Campbell had turned around and caught her, he hadn't been surprised to see her. He'd known she was there and had wanted her to hear, probably so she wouldn't fall in love with Ash and be hurt when he couldn't return her feelings. Special Agent Campbell really was the protector everyone thought he was. The only problem was that his protection had come too late. When Ash had been injured in the alley, Claire had been forced to admit she was starting to have feelings for him.

But now she had proof—his own words—that she was nothing to him and would never be.

"You've got to stop sneaking away from me," Reyes admonished her as he pushed her the last few feet through the doorway into Ash's room.

"Maybe if you hadn't been flirting with those nurses, you wouldn't have lost her," Maggie said as she joined them.

"I was protecting your baby from being fawned all over," Reyes said.

"By offering yourself up to be fawned over?" the dark-haired woman scoffed.

He grinned. "Hey, it would've worked if your kid wasn't so damn cute."

"The baby is adorable," Claire agreed. She'd thought she only needed someone with whom to share her life—a man who shared her interests and her passions. But now she realized she wanted it all. She wanted what Maggie Campbell had—the man and the child. She wanted a family.

But she knew without a doubt now that Ash wouldn't meet any of her needs.

"How are you?" he asked her.

"Fine," she replied even though she felt completely empty inside with her hope gone. But she forced a smile and added, "Now that I'm off my ankle. How's your leg?"

"Not bad, except for the hole. Guess we won't be going dancing for a while," Ash said.

She doubted that they would ever go dancing again.

"But it'll be fine," he added, as if trying to reassure her.

He was a freaking legend—if she believed Reyes. So of course he would be fine. She would be fine, too, when she got over the stupid crush she'd developed on the FBI agent who had only been doing his job.

"Your leg is not going to heal overnight," Reyes cautioned him. "You're going to have to take it easy."

Ash shook his head. "I can't."

"You have no choice."

He stared hard at Reyes and asked, "What are you telling me?"

"Agent in charge assigned someone else to protect Ms. Molenski."

Anger glinted in Ash's blue eyes as he said, "I'm the agent in charge of this assignment."

"The agent in charge of the Bureau," Reyes clarified. "Chief Special Agent Lynch assigned someone else to protection duty."

Ash glared at him now. "Let me guess. You?"

Reyes shook his head. "I don't do protection duty, either." He pointed toward Ash lying in the hospital bed. "I wouldn't want to get distracted and wind up with a bullet in my leg." He glanced over at Blaine and the man's wife and baby and he moved his body in an exaggerated shudder of revulsion. "Or a family…"

Instead of taking offense, Blaine and Maggie laughed. And Maggie told him, "You're going to change your mind one day."

He shook his head. "Never going to happen."

"Never say never," Blaine warned him.

He hadn't offered Ash the same warning, probably because he knew Ash so well that he knew the man was unlikely to change his mind.

"Who's going to protect Claire?" Ash wanted to know.

"The chief assigned a female agent," Reyes said. "He must've thought Ms. Molenski is so beautiful that she would distract any man."

Claire laughed at Reyes's outrageous flirting. "You're crazy."

"Yes," Blaine agreed. "So it's a good thing he wasn't assigned your protection duty."

"He shouldn't have assigned anyone else," Ash said, his voice gruff with resentment.

"It's a good thing," Reyes said. "Neither of you are in any condition to outrun hired thugs right now. And the agent he's assigning is really good. But she won't be the only one. There'll be backup, too."

But there wouldn't be Ash. After overhearing what she had, she should have been relieved. Instead she was disappointed that she would have no excuse to see him anymore. But not seeing him might make it easier for her to get over her crush.

"I'd like a minute alone with Claire," Ash told his friends.

"Sure," Reyes said. "Say your goodbyes and I'll bring Ms. Molenski to her new safe house."

Another place. Another agent. Claire felt nothing but resignation now. Her life had been turned upside down, but this time it had been through no fault of her own.

He waited until it was just the two of them before he spoke. "I'm sorry."

Had he realized that she'd overheard him telling his friend that he didn't need anybody and never would?

"For what?" she asked.

"For putting you in danger."

"You're not the one who offered that information up

for sale," she said. That was the person who'd put her in danger—somebody she apparently knew.

"But I took advantage of the situation," he said. "I took advantage of you."

He hadn't but she almost wished that he had—that she had more memories of them than just their kissing and their dancing. But if they had made love, she would have fallen completely and probably irrevocably in love with him.

"You saved my life," she reminded him. "I'm fine."

"Put up the posting that you initially wanted to," he urged her. "Make sure that nobody thinks you're the one who offered that information."

She shrugged. "Does it matter?" she wondered. "People will think what they will. I am the hacker who managed to get around all those firewalls."

"But you fixed the security problems," he said.

She appreciated that he believed her. "I hope I did. But there might be a better hacker who found a new way around those firewalls."

She'd been too proud and maybe too arrogant to consider that when he had suggested it before. But she had to admit that it was an actual possibility. There were always new hackers with new methods. She worked with quite a few.

"Don't worry about that," he said. "Just concentrate on staying safe."

"We both know that I won't be safe until the person who really offered that information for sale is caught," she said. Since she probably worked with that person, she should be able to figure out who it was.

"Don't," Ash said as if he'd read her mind. "Don't try to investigate on your own."

"I won't be alone," she said. "I'll have protection."

But she wouldn't have him. She worried that no one could keep her as safe as Ash had. But while he'd protected her life, he had endangered her heart. Without him, her heart might be safe. But what about her life?

Chapter Sixteen

A week had passed without another attempt on Claire's life. Ash should have been relieved, especially since he had been laid up in the hospital most of that week. His leg was healed now, at least well enough that he could walk with only a limp and a twinge or more of pain.

"I can get back to the assignment," Ash told the Bureau chief. He had requested this meeting in the man's office in Chicago. Unfortunately the chief had called in Dalton Reyes and Blaine, too.

He wasn't sure who they were supposed to back up. Him or the chief. Since they were supposed to be his friends, he hoped it was him.

"From what I gather, you haven't left it," Chief Special Agent Lynch remarked.

Ash glanced at his friends or the men he'd thought were his friends. What had they told his boss?

"You've been working leads—" his boss reminded him of the reports Ash had been giving him "—trying to track down more buyers and the potential seller of the national security information."

"I've been working from a laptop," Ash clarified, which had frustrated the hell out of him. He'd wanted another meeting with Peter Nowak to see if the former CIA agent was really as above suspicion as the rest of the world seemed to think. He'd also wanted to talk to Leslie Morrison. But most of all he'd wanted to see Claire to make sure that she was healed and healthy and happy. "But the doctor has cleared me to return to fieldwork."

The chief glanced at the letter Ash had given him from his doctor. "Was that in another letter?" he asked. "Because I'm not reading that in this one. I'm reading that you're not completely healed and that you can only return to restricted duty."

"I can return to full duty," Ash insisted. "The restrictions are just a recommendation and totally unnecessary. I'm fully recovered."

"Do you want to return to full duty?" Chief Lynch asked. "Or do you want to return to Claire Molenski?"

Now he glared at the other agents; they had betrayed his friendship if they had told their boss that he had feelings for Claire. But just the mention of her name had his heart rate quickening. "She's in danger."

"Is she?" Reyes asked. "It's been a week with no other attempts to abduct her."

That could have been because Claire had posted that she had no way to bypass government or bank firewalls—if she had actually posted as much. Ash hadn't found any such post, though. Was that because she thought people wouldn't believe it? Or because she'd wanted to continue flushing out terrorists and other radicals?

"She's barely left her office, though," Ash pointed out. "And with the increased security at the consultation company, it would be hard for anyone to abduct her from there."

The chief raised a brow. "And how do you know her whereabouts of the past week?"

"I've stayed involved in the assignment," he admitted what the chief already knew.

Lynch glanced at Reyes and Blaine, his dark eyes narrowed with suspicion. Maybe that was why he'd called them into the meeting. Not because of what they'd told Lynch but because of what they'd told Ash. They had kept eyes on Claire, making sure for him that she truly was safe.

"Why?" the chief asked.

"Because it's my job," Ash explained, "to find who the real risk to national security is. I need to get back out in the field."

"Back out in the field or back to Claire Molenski?" Lynch asked.

He had to see Claire. A week without seeing her beautiful face, without hearing her snarky comments had seemed like never-ending emptiness.

"Claire works with whoever the real risk is," Ash said. "And I've established a cover as her boyfriend. I can resume that undercover assignment."

"You're not in physical condition for protection duty," the chief said as he tapped a fingertip against the doctor's letter.

"I don't do protection duty," Ash said. "I'm undercover. And I'll have backup." He glanced to his friends again.

"They're not in your division," the chief pointed out.

"You're the one who invited them to this meeting," Ash said.

The chief sighed. "A case like this does involve organized crime and bank security. That's why Reyes has already been working it and why Special Agent Campbell should be working it, too."

"I should be working it again, too," Ash insisted.

Lynch chuckled now with amusement. "You sound

like a wounded athlete trying to get back on the court too early." And he was the coach, refusing to let him play.

"It's not too early," Ash said. In fact, he hoped it wasn't too late. There might not have been another abduction attempt in the past week but that didn't mean that one wasn't in the planning stages. Or that the real hacker hadn't decided to stop Claire from finding out his identity.

Because Ash had no doubt that she was trying to find out who it was—that was why she was spending so much time at the office. She hadn't even come to the hospital to see him again, hadn't called. She hadn't even taken his calls when he'd checked in with the agent assigned her protection duty now.

Lynch sighed. "You're a good agent, Stryker, so I'm trusting you to know your limitations."

He knew his limitations. That was how he knew he wasn't the man for whom Claire had been looking at the speed dating event. She needed a man who wanted to be a boyfriend, who wanted to someday be a husband and a father. He'd seen the way she'd looked at Blaine's baby—with longing. She wanted a baby. She wanted a family.

Ash couldn't give her anything she needed besides his protection. And truthfully, he wasn't sure how capable he was of that since he wasn't one hundred percent physically.

"Don't overdo it," Lynch advised him, "and put yourself or an asset like Ms. Molenski in danger."

"I'll be fine," Ash assured him. And he tried to conceal his limp as he walked out of the man's office.

Blaine and Reyes followed him, Reyes grinning as he caught his flinch. "You're fine, my ass," he murmured.

"I've been hurt worse than this before," Ash said and looked to Blaine for confirmation.

"Physically, yeah," Blaine agreed.

"What else is there?" Reyes asked with the oblivion of a man who'd never had an emotional loss.

But Ash's loss had been a long time ago. So he doubted that was what his friend was talking about now. He raised a brow in silent question.

"Claire may not want to see you again," Blaine warned him.

Panic clutched Ash's heart. "Why not?"

"She was there," he said, "when you were talking about how you never needed anyone and never would."

"Why would she care that he was talking smack?" Reyes asked.

"Because she cares about Ash," Blaine said.

Ash shook his head in doubt. If she cared, why hadn't she checked with him to see how he was doing, if his gunshot wound was healing?

"Claire was only playing along as part of the cover," Ash said. And because she'd wanted dating experience so that she could find someone who was an actual match for her.

It wasn't him. They both knew it.

But Ash couldn't forget how well they'd danced together, how perfectly she had fit in his arms. He couldn't forget kissing her, either, the silkiness and the warmth of her lips beneath his.

But he wasn't her boyfriend. He wasn't even her bodyguard. He was just an FBI agent who wanted to make sure she was safe. But he had a sick feeling, an eerie sense of foreboding that she wasn't safe, that she needed him...

So he headed straight to her office. But nobody sat behind her glass walls. The lights and her computers were off. She'd obviously spent a lot of time there though, because take-out containers overflowed her trash can. They'd fallen on the floor.

But the only thing on her desk besides her monitors was the snow globe her father had given her. It glittered slightly in the light shining in from the hall.

"She's gone," a deep voice informed him.

Ash turned toward Peter Nowak and asked, "Did she quit?" He'd met the man a couple of times over the years, most recently when he'd begun investigating the threat. Of course the Bureau chief had been present then, so Ash hadn't been able to ask him the questions he'd wanted to ask him.

The silver-haired man laughed. "No. She just left early today." He lowered his voice. "With her security detail. She's fine."

"Is she?" Ash wondered. "She's nearly been kidnapped a few times. She's been hurt."

Nowak glanced down at Ash's leg. "You, too. But that's part of the job."

He would know. It was an injury that had taken the former CIA agent out of the field.

"It's part of my job," Ash agreed. "It shouldn't be part of hers."

Nowak sighed. "I never intended to put her in danger."

Ash tensed. Was the man making an admission of guilt? Was he the one selling out?

The older man pressed a hand against his suit jacket, over his heart, as if wounded by the suspicion on Ash's face. "Because I gave her the highest clearance. That's all I meant about putting her in danger."

"But she doesn't have the highest clearance," Ash noted. "You do."

Nowak glared, angry now instead of offended. "You

don't want to make an enemy of me, Agent Stryker," he warned him. "I have far more friends in the Bureau than you do."

Was that how he'd been eliminated so quickly as a suspect? Because of his friends?

"I'm not the one who should be worried about my career," Ash said. "You're the one whose company and reputation is at stake right now."

"Exactly," Nowak pointed out. "I wouldn't have risked either. Someone else is behind this, but you're so busy suspecting the wrong people that you haven't found the right suspect." The first time they'd met, the man had defended Claire, had said that Ash was wrong about her.

He'd been right then. And he was right now about Ash being worried. He wasn't worried about his career, though. He was worried about Claire. Maybe she'd left early because she had found the right suspect.

He had to find her before she put herself in more danger than she already was.

CLAIRE HAD SPENT the past week at the office. But no matter how much she'd thrown herself into her work, she hadn't gotten any closer to finding who was behind the information auction.

Nor had she forgotten about Ash…

She had wanted to call him. Or at least take his calls when he'd checked in with the agent protecting her. But she hadn't trusted herself not to betray her feelings for him.

Agent Sally Burnham already suspected that Claire had a crush on her former protector. Mostly because she had one on Agent Stryker herself. When they'd first met, the woman had expressed jealousy over his posing as Claire's boyfriend.

"I wish he was mine," the woman had dreamily commented.

Claire had shared that wish, but she'd only admitted it to herself. Then she'd focused on work. That hadn't been possible today, though, because Martin hadn't showed up.

Martin always showed up. He never called in sick. No matter how hungover or sleep deprived, the young man had never missed a day. Nor had he ever failed to answer his cell when Claire texted or called.

He hadn't come in today, not even late. And he hadn't answered any of her texts or calls. So she had convinced Agent Burnham to bring her by Martin's apartment.

"This might not have been a good idea," Burnham admitted as she peered around the run-down neighborhood. She reached under her jacket, probably for her weapon, but she didn't pull it out.

Apparently Nowak Computer Consulting didn't pay assistants that well if the dilapidated apartment complex was all Martin had been able to afford. Sirens wailed but didn't drown out the loud music and the shouting emanating from several apartments as Claire and Agent Burnham walked down the dirty hallway to Martin's unit. Technically, Burnham walked slowly while Claire limped. Her ankle was healing since she had spent most of the past week with it propped up on a chair.

It was starting to hurt now and she had to be careful to not twist it again on the stuff strewn around the hallway. Empty beer cans, liquor bottles and fast-food bags lined the floor like breadcrumbs leading them farther down the hall.

"We have to check on him," Claire insisted. "Martin sometimes drinks too much."

Maybe he'd gotten alcohol poisoning. Or had been robbed since his neighborhood wasn't the safest.

Her worry increasing, she hurried down to the door of his apartment and lifted her hand to knock. But Agent Burnham caught her wrist and stopped her.

The dark-haired woman had drawn her weapon now, and she held it tightly in her other hand. "We have backup coming," she said. "We should wait."

But the same uneasy feeling that had compelled Claire to check up on her assistant made her reluctant to wait a moment longer. What if he was incapacitated inside and needed help?

She couldn't worry about her safety when another person—a person she knew and cared about—possibly needed her. She tugged her wrist free of the other woman's grasp and pounded her knuckles against the door.

The force of her knock had the door creaking open; it wasn't locked. It hadn't even been shut tightly. She couldn't imagine anyone leaving their doors open in this apartment building in this area of the city. Martin was sometimes distracted and out of it, at least when he was hungover. But she couldn't imagine that he would have forgotten to shut or lock his door.

Then she noticed the splintered wood around the door. The jamb was broken. That was why the door wasn't shutting. Someone had either pried it open or kicked it open in their haste to get inside.

"Martin!" she called out, raising her voice above the din of the music and the shouting.

If there was a reply, she couldn't hear it, so she rushed inside the apartment. It was far messier than hers had ever been—furniture overturned, the stuffing from the cushions fluttering about the room like the snow in her globe.

"Martin, are you okay?" she shouted as she stumbled over the broken furniture.

He wasn't. He lay in a pool of blood on the floor, staring up at her through dead eyes. A scream tore from her throat.

Chapter Seventeen

Despite the loud music and the shouting and the sirens, Ash heard Claire's scream. The volume of it cut through the noise; the terror of it cut through his heart. Ignoring the pain radiating from his leg, he ran toward her.

Ignoring the gun that swung toward him as he burst through the doorway, he rushed past the female agent, holstered his gun and grabbed Claire's trembling shoulders.

"Are you all right?" he anxiously asked her.

She shook her head.

"Where are you hurt?" And why the hell hadn't the agent protected her?

"I'm not the one who's hurt," she said as she pointed a shaking hand toward the floor.

And Ash tore his attention from her to focus on the dead man. "Your assistant..."

The man was obviously dead, his eyes open wide in shock and unseeing in death. Blood stained his bleached blond hair. And his face was a swollen mess of fresh bruises. His fingers had also been broken, and his arms and legs were at odd angles from his torso. He had been tortured.

Claire had to know that Martin was more than hurt;

he was gone. Dead. She trembled while tears streamed down her face.

Ash turned toward the female agent again. "Why did you bring her here?"

"When he didn't show up for work or answer her calls, she insisted on coming here," Agent Burnham said.

"You're supposed to be protecting her," Ash admonished the woman. "Instead, you bring her to a murder scene..." One of the most gruesome he'd ever seen. He shuddered at the pain the young man must have endured.

"I insisted," Claire defended the woman. "If she hadn't brought me, I would've come alone." She was still shaking in shock, but she was also bristling with anger and the feistiness he knew and...

He couldn't even think the word. He wouldn't let himself.

"I'm not in FBI custody," she continued. "You can't stop me from going where I want to."

So she could have seen Ash—if she'd wanted. She hadn't wanted to be with him. Instead she had wanted to come here.

"It's too dangerous," he pointed out. Especially in this part of the city.

He had nearly lost it when he'd heard the address where Agent Burnham had brought her. This wasn't an area of the city where anyone should visit, let alone live.

But Martin didn't live anymore.

"What happened?" he asked Burnham.

"We found him that way," the female agent replied.

Actually it looked like Claire had found him that way; she'd entered the apartment first. He wasn't impressed with Agent Burnham's protection duty.

"Did you even check the apartment?" he asked. "To make sure that the killer isn't still here?"

The woman's face reddened with embarrassment, and she finally moved away from the door. But the studio apartment was small. A killer could have only been hiding in the bathroom, and she checked that quickly.

"It's clear," she announced with a shaky sigh of relief.

"Have you called it in?" he asked.

Her face reddened some more, and she hurried into the hall, reaching for her radio.

"It's too late to help him," Claire murmured. She must have mistakenly thought that Ash wanted Burnham to call an ambulance. "I should have come sooner. I should have come when he didn't answer my texts asking why he was late."

And walked in while Martin was being tortured? He shuddered at the thought of what could have happened to her. That *this* could have happened to her, as well. She could have been tortured and killed.

Ash leaned down and felt Martin's skin. He was ice-cold. He shook his head. "I suspect he's been dead for a while," he said. "Maybe since last night. You couldn't have saved him."

Instead of bringing her comfort, his words brought her more tears. They streaked down her face as sobs slipped from her lips. Seeing her in so much pain brought him pain, too. He closed his arms around her and pulled her trembling body against his.

She wrapped her arms around his neck and clung to him. She was scared and upset and only seeking comfort. He knew that her clinging to him wasn't personal; it wasn't like she'd missed him.

Like he had missed her...

He hugged her more tightly and silently thanked God that it wasn't her he'd found dead on the floor. He didn't care what the doctor had recommended. He was going to be the one to keep her safe even if it cost him his life.

CLAIRE'S HEART KEPT pounding erratically. Maybe it was from finding Martin's body. Maybe it was from being with Ash again. He had dismissed Agent Burnham and had brought her home, or at least to the hotel he called home.

He'd settled onto the couch beside her, with his arms encircling her as if he needed to hold her together.

She had felt as though she was falling apart—until he'd pulled her into his arms. Then she'd been able to hang on to him while her world spun out of control.

"My dad and Pam are safe?" she asked. She knew it wasn't the first time she had asked him, but she desperately needed to know.

"Yes," Ash assured her again. "I checked with their security detail, and there have been no threats to their safety. They're going about their honeymoon completely unaware that anyone is even watching them."

She should have been relieved that their lives hadn't been disrupted. But she wasn't entirely convinced that they were really safe—that anyone was really safe right now.

"I didn't know there was any threat to Martin's safety," she murmured miserably. If only she'd known…

"You could talk to your dad and stepmom," Ash offered. "Then you might feel better—"

"No." She shook her head. "No. Someone might trace the call. I couldn't risk it." She couldn't risk their lives any more than she might have already.

"I can make sure that the call isn't traced," he offered.

She considered it for a minute but then shook her head again. "No, my dad would be able to tell that something's wrong." They had always been so close that he would pick up on her fear and sadness. "He would worry, maybe even cut their honeymoon short. I can't do that to them."

"They deserve to be happy," Ash murmured, repeating back words she'd uttered to him what seemed so long ago. "You do, too, Claire."

Tears stung her eyes and her nose. She blinked to fight them back. She had already cried so much all over Ash that his shirt was probably soaked with her tears. But she wanted to cry again because she had no right to happiness. Not now. "No, I don't."

His arms tightened around her as if he sensed she was about to fall apart again. "This wasn't your fault."

"Martin is—was my assistant," she said. "They used him to get to me." She would have closed her eyes to hold in those threatening tears, but then she would see his body again—his poor, brutalized body. He had been tortured like Ash had warned she would be tortured if he hadn't saved her from every single attempt to abduct her.

A horrible thought occurred to her. "What if someone really believes you're my boyfriend?"

"I hope they believe that I am," he said. "Or I've gotten really bad at going undercover."

She shouldn't have agreed to his going undercover as her boyfriend again. She shouldn't have left Martin's apartment with Ash; someone could have seen them. And if someone had, they would assume that they were together. She'd been leaning so heavily on him and not just because her ankle was still sore even though the swelling had gone down.

"But they could use you...like that..." She shuddered as she imagined Ash's handsome face battered and bruised like Martin's had been. "To get to me."

"Don't worry about me," he told her.

As if she could shut off her feelings and concerns so easily.

"You've already been shot trying to save me from a kidnapping attempt," she reminded him and herself of that horror of crawling over to him in the alley and finding him bleeding. "I can't *not* worry about you."

"Then why didn't you come see me again?" he asked. "I was in the hospital a few more days, but you stayed away."

She'd had to force herself to do that. And to do that, she'd forced herself to remember his words—that he had never needed anyone and never would.

"You didn't need me there…"

He groaned. "You overheard me talking to Blaine. He just told me today that he saw you."

Heat rushed to her face. "Eavesdropping. I shouldn't have, but it wasn't like you were saying anything that I didn't already know. I understand that you're just doing your job. And I also understand how much that means to you."

"I'm not just doing my job this time," he said. "I care about you."

Her heart lurched with hope and something else—something she couldn't admit to feeling, even to herself. "I care about you, too," she said. "That's why I don't want you getting hurt again because of me."

"I wasn't hurt because of you and neither was Martin," he said. "I was hurt because of whoever is trying to sell out national security."

"You could be tortured because of that, too," she warned him.

He shrugged. "It wouldn't be the first time. I'm not easy to torture."

The man was a legend. Reyes had already told her

that, but now she believed it herself. "But I don't want to see you like that."

She reached out and slid her palm along his cheek. Light stubble tickled her skin. She shivered in reaction as desire overwhelmed her.

He lowered his head and touched his mouth to hers. But before she could kiss him back, he pulled away. "I'm sorry. You're vulnerable right now."

She had always been vulnerable with him. Before she'd even known who and what he was, he had unsettled her. "This is what I want," she said.

"This?"

"You…" But she couldn't blame him if he didn't want her back. After all the tears she'd wept, her face was probably all swollen and blotchy. How could he want her?

He didn't lower his head to hers again. Instead his arms tightened and he lifted her. Swinging her up, he carried her to the bedroom.

Worried that he was going to lay her down and leave her, she clung to him and pulled him down with her. But he didn't protest. Instead, he kissed her now—passionately. His mouth consumed hers, his lips moving over hers, his tongue dipping inside to taste her.

To devour her.

When he lifted his head again, she panted for breath while her lungs and her heart ached. He levered himself up, and she worried that a kiss was all he was giving her. Again.

But then he pulled off his shirt, along with his holster and his vest. She skimmed her hands over his naked chest, loving every ripple of muscle and soft, dark hair. Then she reached for his belt, pulling it free so that she could lower his zipper.

He groaned.

Then he was undressing her, pulling off her sweater and her jeans and her underwear until she lay naked beneath him. He kissed her again. Her neck, her shoulder, the curve of her breast. His lips closed over a nipple and gently tugged.

She moaned as sensations chased through her body, straight to her core. She ached there, too, for him. "Ash…"

As if he knew, he touched her there. His fingertips teased her while he continued to kiss her breasts and then her lips again.

"Please," she murmured against his mouth as she reached for him. When she closed her hand over his erection, he groaned. "Make love to me," she urged him.

He kept teasing her with his fingers until she squirmed beneath him. And that ache eased slightly as he pleased her. But it wasn't enough. She wanted more. She wanted him—all of him.

She knew she could never have that emotionally, but maybe she could physically. He thrust inside her, building that pressure again with each deliberate stroke. While he moved inside her, he kissed her, their tongues softly caressing each other as their bodies joined in ecstasy.

He was so deep inside her that she felt as if he was part of her—the core of who and what she was. She wrapped her legs around his waist, arching up to meet each thrust. Just as they had on the dance floor, they moved in perfect unison in the bedroom.

After a few more strokes, they reached release together. Claire cried out as the pleasure overwhelmed her. Ash shuddered and then flinched. As he dropped onto his side next to her, she caught sight of the bandage on his thigh. He was not fully recovered from the gunshot wound.

Who had taken advantage of whom?

"I'm sorry," she murmured. Sorry that he'd been hurt. And sorry that he wasn't really her boyfriend.

She was the sorriest that she had already fallen in love with him.

Chapter Eighteen

"I'm the one who should be sorry," Ash said. "I crossed the line."

And despite all the times he had gone undercover before, Ash had never crossed that line. He had always acted professionally even when he'd been acting like a terrorist or a member of a gang or militia.

But for the first time in his career, he had been distracted from his assignment. He had never been distracted in the way that Claire Molenski distracted him.

His gun was on the floor. What if someone had followed them here from her assistant's apartment? Would he have had the presence of mind to hear someone breaking into the hotel suite? Would he have been able to reach his weapon in time to defend her?

"I just about begged you to cross that line," she said, and her face flushed red with embarrassment.

Or passion...

She was such a passionate woman. She had reacted to his every touch so much so that he wanted to touch her again. But she reached out first.

Her fingers trailed over his thigh, along the edge of his bandage. "I forgot that you're still recovering."

"I'm recovered," he assured her, and he wasn't just

talking about his leg as another part of his anatomy reacted to her touch.

She sucked in an audible breath of surprise. "Is that possible?"

"Apparently so…" He had never wanted anyone again as quickly, but maybe that was because he had never wanted anyone as much as he did Claire.

Her fingers trailed up his thigh to his manhood. He gritted his teeth, but still a groan slipped out. Her fingertips skimmed over him, teasing him.

"Claire…"

"You don't want to make love to me again?" she asked, and she actually fluttered her lashes at him. He'd seen Claire sassy and scared; he'd never seen her flirting. The woman was dangerous. So very dangerous to him…

His heart shifted in his chest, lurching as it swelled with emotion. But he refused to give a name to all those surging emotions. He would only recognize and act on the passion as he made love to her again.

He made love to her thoroughly, kissing her lips and every inch of her silky skin. She writhed beneath him, arching her hips, begging for more.

She forgot his injury again. She forgot her pain and loss. Maybe she was just using him to forget that she'd lost a friend. Ash didn't care.

He would do whatever he could to ease her pain. So he gave her pleasure instead, loving her over and over… until her tears began to fall again. He tensed, but it was too late—his pleasure came—overpowering him so much that he felt close to tears himself.

He was overwhelmed and humbled. And all he could do was hold her close as she sobbed onto his chest.

THE NEXT FEW days passed in a blur of emotion and regret and loss. Claire had spent enough time in the hotel suite—enough time in Ash's arms—crying, making love, falling in love...

Or she had probably fallen in love earlier before they had even made love. Maybe it had happened on the dance floor. Or in the alley.

But it didn't really matter *when* she'd fallen. It didn't even matter *that* she had fallen—because nothing would ever come of her feelings. While Ash had made love with her, he wasn't in love with her.

She doubted that he was even capable of falling in love since he was so convinced that he had never needed and would never need anyone. All he wanted was his career.

Not a wife or family. Not even a real girlfriend...

While she loved Ash Stryker, she knew he wasn't the man for her—not the man with whom she could spend her life. She would never have with him what her father had with Pam. Or Leslie had with Ed.

And she wanted it all.

At the moment none of that mattered, though. She cared about nothing but paying her respects. So she stepped out of the bedroom in a black dress.

Ash glanced up from his computer and his body tensed as he studied what she was wearing. "Where do you think you're going?" he asked.

She tensed then. "This isn't any dancing dress," she pointed out. "So I think you know..."

He shook his head. "You can't."

"I can't *not* go," she said.

"It's too dangerous."

That was what he'd said every time she had attempted to leave the apartment over the past few days. It was too dangerous.

And after seeing Martin's battered body, she hadn't argued with him. She had even ordered her black dress online since she hadn't wanted to go out to buy it. But she had every intention of going out to wear it.

"I don't care how dangerous it is," she said. "I have to do this."

"Why?"

"I need to pay my respects," she said.

But she wasn't even certain who she would pay them to; she didn't know if her assistant had any family. He hadn't talked about his parents or siblings. He had mentioned friends, ones he'd partied with. But she really needed to pay her respects to Martin himself.

"This isn't about respect," Ash said. "It's about regret. You blame yourself for what happened to Martin."

She couldn't deny that.

"What if I do?" she asked. "It makes no difference in this situation. I still need to go to the funeral." Actually, she needed to go even more because she felt so responsible for what the poor kid had endured. It was bad enough that he'd died, but how he'd died...

She shuddered at the horrific memories.

Ash shook his head again in refusal. He had apparently forgotten that she didn't need his permission. She wasn't in his custody, only his protection.

"Martin was my friend," she said. But maybe that was stretching it.

Ash called her on that exaggeration. "Did you hang out at his apartment? Did you go to the bars he went to?"

She said nothing and just glared at him.

"Did you have him over to your apartment?" he asked. "For dinner? To watch a movie?"

"I didn't have to go out with him," she said. "We were work friends. I saw him every day for the past three years." That was more than she'd seen anyone else, even her father.

Ash sighed. "Just because you worked with the man doesn't make you friends."

She laughed at his hypocrisy. "So you're not friends with Agent Campbell and Agent Reyes?"

"I am," he said. "But Blaine and I knew each other longer before we worked for the Bureau. And Reyes and I have a lot in common."

She hadn't known Martin well enough to know if they'd had anything in common. "It doesn't matter if we were real friends or not." After she'd been busted for hacking, she had been too busy to keep old friends or to make new ones. "He was my assistant and I'm going to his funeral."

Ash sighed in resignation as he put aside his laptop and stood up. He only flinched a little as he put weight on his wounded leg. Like her sprained ankle, it was healing quickly.

"This is a bad idea," he warned her.

Maybe it was.

"You're wearing a suit," she remarked. "Are you going to the office?"

He shook his head. "No. I know you," he said. "I knew you'd want to go to the funeral no matter my telling you how bad an idea this is."

"You knew?" He knew her well. But unfortunately, she knew him well, too. So well that she'd had to accept they had no future together.

He sighed again—a long-suffering sigh as if protecting her was such a chore. But then given what he'd been through, it was.

"And you intend to go with me?" she asked.

His lips curved into a slight grin. "What kind of boy-friend would I be if I let you go to a funeral alone?"

"A real one?"

"You must have had some really lousy boyfriends," he remarked.

"I haven't dated for a long time," she said. So she couldn't remember what her boyfriends had been like, but apparently they hadn't stood by her when she'd gotten in trouble for hacking.

Ash nodded in recollection. "That was why you wanted my kisses."

His blue eyes brightened and glistened with desire. He must have been remembering that he'd given her more than kisses. She'd wanted that, too.

But she didn't want this, didn't want him acting like a real boyfriend, because he might get hurt again.

"I already called Agent Burnham," she said. "She can go with me."

The brightness of his eyes dimmed. "Hell, no."

"It wasn't her fault that I went to Martin's apartment." That she'd found him…

"No," he agreed. "It was yours. Just like going to this funeral is your mistake."

Her anger flared like it had when he'd suggested that there could be a better hacker than her. He hurt her pride more than anyone she'd ever known—probably because she cared so much what he thought of her. She needed to stop caring about him. "Fine. It's my mistake. I'll make it alone."

She headed toward the door, but he stepped between it and her, blocking her exit. He was close—so close that she felt his breath when he murmured, "You're not going anywhere…"

Her heart pounded harder as she wondered if he

intended to carry her back to the bedroom like he had a few days ago. He'd made love to her then to distract her from her pain. From what she'd seen.

She wasn't going to let him distract her again—not that he had tried since that first night. She'd awakened alone the morning after they'd made love, and for the most part, except for a glance he shot her now and then, he'd acted as if it hadn't happened. As if they hadn't made love.

That had hurt her pride and made her mad at him, too. "I'm not?" she challenged his order—or at least his right to give her any orders.

"You're not going anywhere alone," he continued. "I'm going with you."

But she wasn't pacified.

She would rather go alone than put him in danger. But she had to do this.

For Martin.

She had already cost the young man his life. It was her expertise that Martin had been tortured to divulge. So, no matter how Ash tried to convince her otherwise, it was her fault.

She shrugged. "Suit yourself, suit…"

She knew Ash well enough to know that he would anyway. If she refused to go to the funeral with him, he would show up alone.

"It's your funeral," she warned him and then flinched at her poor choice of words. It wasn't his funeral. At least it wasn't yet.

He turned the knob and held open the door for her. "I just hope it doesn't wind up being yours."

She waited until she passed him before murmuring, "Me, too…"

She didn't want it to be his funeral, either. Hopefully

he had called in his friends—his real friends—for reinforcements. Because she had a bad feeling that they might need them.

Chapter Nineteen

Ash walked into the funeral home with one arm clamped tightly around Claire. To anyone watching them—and a lot of people watched them—it could have looked as if her boyfriend was offering her emotional support. Instead he was trying to protect her. That was why he held her with only one arm, so that his other hand was free to grab his gun from the holster under his suit jacket.

Claire thought her assistant had been killed to get to her. If that was true, then his funeral would be the perfect place to actually get to her. Because anyone who knew Claire would know that she would have to pay her respects to her young assistant. Even now she moved down the aisle of the funeral home toward the casket sitting in front of the room.

Ash wasn't convinced that Martin deserved her respects. She felt guilty—as though she was the one who'd put her assistant in danger. Ash was beginning to believe that it might have been the other way around.

The kid hadn't possessed the hacker skills that Claire had. According to Nowak's background check in Martin's employee file, he had only hacked in to some video games and a few social media sites, so he couldn't have found ways around bank and government firewalls. He couldn't have been selling his own knowledge. But maybe he'd been selling hers.

After seeing where he'd lived, it was obvious Martin had needed money. When Ash had conducted a deeper investigation into the kid's financials, he had found that Martin had debts, too. Gambling debts. And those kinds of people, bookies and loan sharks, didn't like waiting for their money.

"This was a bad idea," warned the voice in his ear— through the radio device. Dalton Reyes's voice merely echoed the voice already in Ash's head telling him he'd made a mistake. "I recognize a lot of these people…"

From organized crime. Just whom had Martin borrowed from for those gambling debts? Who did he owe? And had they showed up to try to collect from whoever had survived Martin and inherited those debts?

Ash recognized some faces himself—from terrorism watch lists. That posting could have brought out all of them. He suspected one of them had probably tortured Martin. Had the kid admitted that he knew nothing? But before he'd died, had he given up Claire, exposing her as the only one who could have bypassed those firewalls?

"We should go," Ash told her as they stopped at the open casket. The kid looked better now—with his eyes closed and makeup covering his wounds—than he had when Claire had found him. Maybe she'd needed this, needed an image to superimpose over that other, more horrific one in her mind. She didn't need to stay for the services, though. "You're not safe here."

She trembled against him. He felt and heard her uneven breathing. She was crying again. He hated how much pain she was in over her assistant's death, and he hated that coming to this funeral would only cause her more pain emotionally.

And probably physically, as well.

"We don't have enough backup," Reyes warned in his ear. "We have to get the hell out of here."

They had prepared for the possibility of a few suspects attending Martin's funeral, like Leslie Morrison and Peter Nowak; Leslie sat next to his former employer in chairs a couple rows back from the casket. By seeing them together, conversing in hushed tones, Ash realized that Leslie wasn't a former employer. He still worked for Nowak.

Ash had pored over all the employee records, though, so Leslie's capacity wasn't official. What did he unofficially do for Nowak that the two of them looked so guilty to be caught together?

Their faces flushed as they caught him staring at them. Then their gazes went to Claire, and that look of guilt increased. Had their greedy plan put her in danger? Were they concerned that she might wind up like her assistant had? Lying in a casket, tortured and dead?

Ash had to make certain that she didn't wind up that way. The Bureau hadn't prepared for as many suspects as had showed up for the funeral; they were outgunned.

"We need to leave," Ash told Claire. He turned her around before Leslie and her boss could approach her.

He expected her to dig in her heels, like Edith had when her husband had tried to move her away on the dance floor. He expected Claire to argue that she couldn't leave until after the service.

But she offered him no argument. Instead she moved quickly, despite her still-swollen ankle, down the aisle between all those "mourners." She was a smart woman. He should have known that she would realize the danger they were in.

He just hoped that they hadn't realized it too late.

HAD ANYONE REALLY cared about Martin? Nobody cried. The only one who had shed a tear for him had been Claire. But those tears dried as she realized what Ash probably already had. Maybe she had already known, too, but hadn't wanted to face it until now. Until she saw that there really weren't any mourners at the funeral…

Except for Leslie and her boss and a few kids that must have partied with Martin, the rest of the mourners were scary goons in ill-fitting suits. Ill-fitting because the suits couldn't completely hide the weapons beneath their jackets. These guys looked like the men who had already tried abducting Claire. They were hired hench-men. Or buyers.

Martin was the one; he had posted that information for sale. But he hadn't had the actual knowledge. Un-like Leslie, who had mentored her, she hadn't taught the young man everything she knew—probably because she hadn't completely trusted him. And apparently with good reason. But had he been trying to sell her knowledge anyway?

Was he the one who'd put her in danger?

It certainly appeared so as those scary men closed in around her. They reached for her now as she and Ash tried to push through the crowd gathering around her.

The people were like paparazzi, pushing close for a picture. But they didn't just want a picture. They wanted Claire.

For three years Martin had been her assistant, and he had betrayed her.

Was there anyone else she could trust?

Ash.

She clung to him. But he was easing away from her slightly. Then she realized why when he pulled his weapon and blew his cover.

"FBI Special Agent Stryker," he said. "Step back."

Instead of warning the men away, his announcement seemed to free them to pull their own weapons. Screams and shouts of fear rose from the few real mourners.

Claire couldn't scream. Her fear was choking her. But she wasn't afraid just for herself. She was afraid for Ash, too. He was still recovering from his previous gunshot wound. He couldn't get shot again.

She had been wrong. So wrong to insist on attending this funeral. As he'd warned her, it would probably wind up being hers. And his.

She cleared her throat just enough to whisper to him, "I'm sorry…"

She wanted to tell him more. She wanted to tell him that she loved him. She had held those words back before, out of embarrassment, because she'd known that they were too incompatible to have a future together. Now she realized they had no future at all.

But before she could say anything more, gunfire erupted in the funeral home. The shots were close and deafening. Claire covered her ears as Ash covered her body with his.

He wore a vest, but it hadn't mattered last time. He had still been shot. She doubted it would protect him any better this time. He'd taken a bullet in the leg before; she suspected these men would aim for his head. They would want him dead quickly so that they could get to her.

She wanted to apologize again. Most of all, she wanted to profess her feelings.

But it was too late.

ASH WASN'T EVEN certain who was firing. The bad guys or his backup. No matter who was shooting, the bullets were going wild, endangering everyone inside the building. He needed to get Claire out of the funeral home.

He kept low, covering her with his body, and led her toward the exit. But hands grabbed at him. He swung his gun in every direction, but he only fired to stop the other men from firing at him.

He wasn't worried about his own life but Claire's and what would happen to her once he was no longer able to protect her. Even now pain radiated throughout his healing leg, but he ignored it as he pushed forward.

She wobbled on her feet—maybe with fear. Maybe with pain from her healing ankle. He shouldn't have brought her here. But he'd thought he'd had enough backup.

Now in the chaos, he didn't even know who was the backup and who was the threat. So he trusted no one but the voice in his head warning him to get out as quickly as possible.

And Reyes's voice telling him which direction to take like he had when all those panel vans had surrounded him on the streets.

"Go out the side door," the other agent advised. "You won't get out the way you came in—except in a body bag."

Ash changed direction just in time. The bullets intended for him struck chairs near him as he propelled Claire through the sitting area. He saw no side door.

And for a moment he wondered if he should have trusted that voice in his ear.

By his own admission Dalton Reyes had grown up with thugs. While he had arrested several, he'd also admitted that they'd been his friends. So maybe he still had some allegiance with them. Maybe, for the right price, Reyes could be a thug himself.

But then the door loomed ahead, an emergency exit that wasn't immediately visible behind a potted palm. The long fronds nearly hid the escape route. But it had never been more of an emergency than it was now as hands grabbed at Ash, pulling him back as more hands grabbed at Claire, tugging her away from him.

He slammed his elbow back into some guy's nose. Blood spurted. Then he struck another with the barrel of his gun. With a curse and an oath, the guy dropped to the carpet.

But still Claire was being pulled away from him toward that exit. Had Reyes set him up?

Someone Claire trusted had set her up. Maybe nobody could be trusted now with so much at stake.

Ash could rely only on himself. So he lifted his gun.

The man holding Claire pointed his gun toward her head. "I will kill her," he threatened.

Her green eyes widened with fear. But then she nodded slightly—giving Ash permission to fire. The guy probably didn't intend to really shoot Claire. It had to be only an empty threat since it was her knowledge that everyone wanted. Other people stepped back, too afraid to call his bluff.

But then, even if his threat was empty, he could kill her accidentally since his finger was against the trigger. He could pull it convulsively when he was shot. Using his back, the man pushed open that emergency exit door—intending to drag her outside with him.

A siren wailed, announcing to the room that the door had been opened, that Claire was about to be dragged out. Sirens outside echoed the wail of that siren, as additional reinforcements arrived. But they were too late to be much help anymore.

Even if they got inside quickly, Claire would already

be gone. And, with all the armed men around him, Ash would probably already be dead.

Claire's eyes widened again with shock and disappointment. She had trusted Ash to protect her, to keep her safe.

So he trusted himself, and he took the shot. More gunfire echoed.

Chapter Twenty

Blood dripped down Claire's face and throat and soaked her hair. She couldn't stop shaking; her quivering muscles were beyond her control. She had never felt as powerless as she had in that funeral home, as she did now when she couldn't even control her own body.

Her teeth chattered, and goose bumps raised her chilled skin. She was so cold.

She didn't even feel the warmth when Ash slid his arm around her. She felt nothing anymore but shock...

"You're okay," he soothed her. "You didn't get shot." But his fingers shook as he wiped the blood from her face. "It's not yours."

It wasn't hers. It had come from the man holding her—the man Ash had shot. But when that man had fallen, another had tried to grab her. It had been the scariest nightmare of her life, but it had been real.

And if not for Ash, she wouldn't have survived. She was surprised that she had. Unless...

"Are you sure?" she asked him.

He cupped her face in his bloodstained hands and studied her. "Are you hurt?" he asked, his voice gruff with anxiety. "Do you think any of this blood is yours?"

"It must be," she said. "We both must be bleeding..."

There was blood on Ash. Some trailing from the

corner of his mouth, some more from a scratch on his forehead. It was his. He had been hurt and all because she had stubbornly insisted on attending the funeral of the man who'd betrayed her.

She reached up and touched his mouth with her trembling fingers. "You are."

Before she could, he wiped away the trace of blood from his lips. "I'm fine."

"How?" she wondered. "How in the world are we both not dead?"

A man chuckled. It wasn't Ash; his face was drawn taut with gravity. He looked to be almost in as much shock as she was that they had survived.

If they had…

Special Agent Blaine Campbell stepped out of the shadows of the room to which Ash had brought her. She didn't remember where they were or how they'd gotten there. She didn't even remember how they had actually escaped the funeral home. Alive.

If they really were…

"I've wondered that myself," Blaine Campbell remarked. "There were some situations in Afghanistan that I still don't know how we survived."

Ash shuddered. "This felt a lot like those…like we weren't going to make it."

"Are you sure you're all right?" Blaine asked as he studied his friend.

Ash shook his head. "No, I'm not all right. I'm mad as hell."

Claire sucked in a breath of surprise at the anger in his voice and on his handsome face. But she couldn't blame him for being mad at her. She had insisted on going to that funeral despite all his warnings.

"I'm sorry," she said. She was so sorry for putting him

in danger—for nearly costing him his life. If something had happened to him...

"I'm mad at myself," he told her. "Mad that I took you into a situation I knew would be dangerous."

"It was my fault," she murmured.

He shook his head. "None of it was yours. It was your assistant's."

The man who'd been hired to help her had been the one who'd really put her in danger. She felt like crying again, but she had already cried too many tears over Martin Crouch.

"He offered your knowledge—he offered *you*—for sale," Ash said, and fury shook his voice.

"But he's the one who paid the price," Blaine remarked, "with his life."

Not only had he died, but he'd died painfully. She felt no vindication in that, only regret.

"It's over," she murmured.

"No," Ash corrected her. "It's not over yet. It's not over until everyone wanting that information—wanting *you*—has been apprehended."

"You're not going to catch them all," Blaine warned him.

"I have to," Ash said with grim determination. "If I don't, Claire will never be safe."

Remembering all those hands grabbing at her, she shuddered in revulsion. She couldn't live like that; she couldn't live in a constant state of fear.

His hands were steady as he cupped her face and tipped it up so that her gaze met his. His blue eyes were full of anger and determination and integrity.

"I will catch them," he promised her. "I will make sure you're safe again."

"What about you?" she asked. He had nearly been

killed so many times. If he went after those men again, he was going to be the one in danger.

"I'll be fine," he said, dismissing her fears for his safety. "And so will you. Blaine will protect you. That's why I brought you here."

Blaine shook his head. "This is a bad idea, Ash. You can't go after all of them alone."

"I'm not," he said. "I have Reyes and the agents who were backup at the funeral home."

"The ones who survived," Blaine said. "There were casualties. Wounded. It was like freaking Afghanistan. I should be out there with you like I was back then."

Ash shook his head in refusal.

"Reyes is a damn good agent," Blaine said, which he probably only admitted because the other man wasn't there to hear him. "He can keep her safe."

"Reyes is damn good," Ash agreed. "But he doesn't have a wife and kid, Blaine. You do. That's why you need to stay with Claire."

The blond man looked as though he was about to argue. But he was torn. He obviously loved his family and didn't want to risk never returning to them.

"It's safer here," Ash said. "I made sure no one followed us."

Blaine nodded, taking him entirely at his word. "I did the same."

So she was safe. But what about Ash?

She reached out and grabbed his arm. "Don't go," she pleaded. "Don't do this…"

"I have to," he said. And he knelt before her chair again and took her face in his hands. Staring deeply into her eyes, he said, "Remember everything that I'm doing, I'm doing for you."

She shivered at his ominous tone. "Getting killed?" she asked. "You're doing that for me?"

Instead of answering her, he stood up. Then he flipped on the TV she hadn't even realized was in the same room with her before stepping outside the door with Blaine. He'd probably turned on the TV so that she wouldn't overhear their conversation. Her ears still ringing from the gunfire, she probably wouldn't have been able to hear them anyway.

But she did hear the TV. On the flat screen, her boss spoke to reporters at a news conference. "There is no threat to national security. There is no way around government or corporate firewalls," Peter Nowak assured the press and the world. "Since Ms. Molenski checked the security for those sites, they have been rechecked and reworked several times."

She noticed a man standing among the reporters. But he wasn't pushing a microphone toward Nowak or flashing a camera. Leslie Morrison was just listening. As Ash had suspected, the man hadn't really retired, he was the one who'd rechecked her work. He'd probably been doing it for years.

Peter Nowak continued his press release. "She has no access to those sites nor does she have any access to Nowak Computer Consulting. Because of the threats to her personal safety, she has resigned."

Claire couldn't remember much of what had happened during or immediately after the funeral home. Maybe she had resigned. But she suspected that she had been fired instead.

Did Peter think that she had been involved in Martin's scheme? That they had been working together?

Or did he think her entirely responsible?

A door closed, startling her, so that she forgot about

the television. She didn't really care about her job anymore. She didn't care if she lost it.

"Where is he?" she asked as only Blaine stepped back inside the room with her.

"He's gone," Blaine replied.

"Why did you let him leave?" she asked. He was still hurt and had just barely survived their last ordeal. The blood on his face had been his.

"For the same reason that he let you go to that funeral," Blaine replied. "I knew I couldn't talk him out of it."

No, Claire didn't care about her job anymore. But she cared about Ash. She didn't want to lose him. But then she had never really had him.

THE WAR ZONE had moved from the funeral home to the international terminal at the airport. Despite airport security, gunfire erupted. Shots were exchanged. Bullets struck intended targets. The wounded were brought to the hospital, the survivors into custody.

"These were your people," Reyes remarked as he watched the last of the vehicles pull away. He turned the key in the ignition of his Bureau-issued SUV. While it was FBI, he'd had it customized with spinner rims and paint with glitter in it so that it would blend in on the streets where he had to go. "Now we round up mine."

Ash didn't care whose people were whose. He just wanted them all apprehended. He just wanted Claire safe. Nowak putting out that press release might have helped. If everyone believed what he'd said...

Reyes glanced over at Ash and gestured at his suit. "Not sure you're going to fit in."

Ash touched his jacket lapel and thought of how Claire called him a suit. "I don't want to fit in."

"Really?" Reyes asked. "I thought that was your

thing—fitting in, going undercover so completely that nobody would ever guess that you're not the cover."

That was the problem. Even he had begun to believe that he was really Claire's boyfriend. She didn't believe, though. She had kissed him just to gain expertise to kiss other, more compatible men. And she had made love with him only because she'd been devastated and lost over the gruesome murder of a man she had thought a friend. Of course her definition of *friend* was far more generous than Ash's.

Martin Crouch hadn't been a friend to her.

For a moment, back at the funeral home, Ash had doubted Reyes's friendship. But the man had been there when Ash had needed him. Once Ash had swept Claire out that side door, Reyes had rescued them in a vehicle, speeding away with them before any more shots could be fired. He had saved them then. And he'd had Ash's back at the airport.

But where they were going now was an area as dangerous as any Ash had ever been. "I'm not worried about a cover right now," he said. He was pretty sure none of Reyes's people would buy one anyway. "I'm worried about ending this. I want this to be over."

"Is it ever really over?" Reyes wondered. "Once this assignment ends, another one begins—which is lucky for us, I guess. Or we wouldn't have jobs. There will always be bad people in this world, though."

"There are good people, too," Ash said.

Reyes sighed and revealed a cynicism he usually hid beneath his humor. "I've met more bad."

"I've met Claire," Ash said.

Reyes laughed now. "And that little thing outweighs all the bad?"

Ash tensed with shock and fear as he realized that for

him, she did. She mattered so much more than all the bad things that had happened to him. "Yes."

Reyes cursed colorfully. "You can't be thinking about her now," he warned Ash. "You can't be distracted. I need you to be focused. Or we're not going to make it out of here alive."

Ash had to make it out alive. He had to go back to Claire and tell her how he felt about her. He had to tell her that, while he had never needed anyone before, he needed somebody now. He needed *her*.

DESPITE HER SPRAINED ANKLE, Claire had been pacing since Ash had left. It had felt like days ago. She should have told him then how she'd felt about him. She should have told him she loved him, and she should have made him promise to come back to her.

The doorknob rattled. Blaine drew his weapon from his holster and stepped between the door and Claire. With his free hand, he gestured her back—indicating she should take cover in the other room of the two-room suite.

But she shook her head, refusing to budge. Sure, it could have been someone else—someone who might have followed them from the funeral home or might have followed Blaine from wherever he'd come. But it could have been Ash.

And she wanted to see him. She needed to see him. Desperately.

"Don't shoot," a deep voice warned before the door opened to a dark-haired man. But it wasn't Ash.

"Reyes," Blaine said, his voice deep with relief.

But Reyes was alone. So Claire felt no relief—only more fear.

"Where is he?" she anxiously asked. "Where's Ash?"

Blaine tensed, too. "What the hell happened, Reyes?"

Now she noticed that the man wasn't as cocky and carefree as he usually was. His dark hair was mussed, his face bruised. He had obviously been in a fight.

With bad guys? Or with Ash?

After Martin's betrayal, Claire had wondered who she should trust. Only Ash...

But he wasn't here; she was alone with these men instead. Ash had trusted these two special agents and considered them his friends. Were they?

"Biggest roundup of bad guys *ever*," Reyes said like a little boy who'd caught the most fish on an outing with his dad and brothers. Or with the enthusiasm of a man who loved what he did.

Blaine must have thought he looked more like a little boy bragging because he chuckled in amusement.

"You're going to be safe now," Reyes told Claire. "It's over."

"It's really over?" she asked doubtfully.

He nodded.

"Then where's Ash?" Why hadn't he come back to tell her? "Is he hurt?"

Reyes touched his lip. Maybe Ash had been the one who'd hit him. "He wasn't when I saw him last."

"What the hell happened?" Blaine asked again.

"He asked me who a gambler would owe money to on my side of the city."

"Martin was a gambler..." She hadn't thought his little bets had been all that serious. But he must have accumulated some debts with the wrong people. Remembering how horrible he had looked when he'd died, she realized it was very serious. Serious enough that he'd been driven to offer her knowledge for sale to save himself.

"You told him?" Blaine asked. "It could be the person who killed Claire's assistant."

"Ash is convinced it is who killed the kid." Reyes touched his swollen lip again. "I offered to bring him there. But he insisted on going alone."

For her? To make sure Martin got justice? But Martin had started everything, had caused so many other deaths and near-deaths. Maybe Martin had had justice.

Tears stung her eyes. But she wasn't crying for the loss of her friend. Her tears were for Ash. "He's confronting a killer alone?"

"Ash has been my friend since we were just a couple of cocky kids in boot camp," Blaine said.

"Some things never change," Reyes murmured.

As if Reyes hadn't spoken, Blaine continued, "But he's always been a loner."

Because he had learned at a young age to trust no one since his parents had been willing to sacrifice his life along with so many others…

Had anyone ever really loved him like she loved him? She should have told him. But she wondered if it would have mattered. Ash cared more about his job and justice than love and relationships.

He had friends, but when he really needed them most, he pushed them away—like he'd pushed her away. Would he survive this confrontation with a killer?

"You know where he went," she pointed out, "so go there. Save him."

But even as she said it, she knew that by the time they arrived it would be too late. Someone would probably already be dead.

She just hoped it wasn't Ash.

Chapter Twenty-One

Ash should have been afraid or at least on edge as he walked into the business of the most notorious loan shark in the seediest part of Chicago. Maybe he wasn't uneasy, though, because it wasn't housed in the usual strip club or pool house from which loan sharks usually worked. This loan shark worked out of a tea shop.

This tea shop took bets and processed high interest loans with just as much frequency as the others. He also had to show his FBI badge to the two goons posted outside before he was even allowed through the doors. He expected them to reach for the guns holstered beneath their lumpy jackets. Or maybe just slam their already battered fists into him. Instead, they opened the stained-glass double doors for him.

Maybe they had already spotted his backup parked across the street. While he had refused to let Reyes come along for the takedown, he wasn't completely careless or stupid. He wasn't going in entirely alone. Given the size of the goons and their guns, it was good that he had backup close. But the guys just nodded as he passed through the doors he held. Maybe they were so passive because they knew that it was all over.

That was why Ash hadn't wanted Reyes along. It was

more important that the other agent go to Claire and assure her that her ordeal was over, that she was finally safe again. Ash never wanted her to be as scared as she'd been in the funeral home or as shocked as she'd been after it.

He'd been so scared that the blood on her face had been hers, that she'd been hit when he'd killed the man holding her. She had stared at Ash so vacantly, but then it had all been too much for her.

As he crossed the hardwood floor of the beautiful little shop, a woman glanced up from her table at the back of the restaurant. She put down her Bunco cards and slid her cat-eye glasses from the end of her nose until they dangled from the thick gold chain around her neck. She wore a sweatshirt like his grandmother would have worn—one with cats on it made of felt or velvet or something. The sweatshirts were about all he remembered of his grandmother; she hadn't approved of his mother, so he hadn't seen her very often.

He suspected this woman would have liked his mother. They were quite alike—every bit as cold-blooded.

"Did you finally give up on that little pale blonde?" she asked hopefully. She hadn't been at the speed dating event to meet anyone; she'd been there to bid on the information Martin had told her was being sold to pay his debts.

Even though Ash had no intention of giving up on Claire, he nodded. "I realized she had nothing for sale. Have you realized the same yet?"

She uttered a heavy sigh of utter resignation. It was probably why her goons hadn't tried to stop him because *she* knew it was over. According to Reyes, Beverly Holdren had run a lucrative loan shark business for many years. She'd had people hurt but never killed. But Martin's wild claim had made her so greedy that she'd crossed a line she'd never crossed before. "Yes."

"Too bad for Martin Crouch that you hadn't realized it sooner."

She narrowed her eyes and stared up at him as if she needed her glasses back on to see him clearly. Or maybe she was just trying to determine how much he knew.

Since she'd fallen for Martin's bluff, he made one of his own. "We have DNA evidence from the scene." The lab hadn't finished processing any of that evidence collected from the scene. He made a tsking noise with his tongue. "It was a very messy scene."

And it was too damn bad that Claire had been the first one to come upon it. She'd been in shock that day, too. She'd been through entirely too much and part of that had been because of this woman.

"Martin...disappointed me," she said, like a grandmother might talk about her naughty grandson.

But a grandmother would have only scolded or at the most paddled his behind. She'd had the poor kid tortured. Maybe she'd even done some of it herself...

"There was a lot of evidence left behind at the scene," Ash added to his bluff. He had no idea what had been collected. "Once we match that DNA to you and your goons, we will have enough for an arrest and a conviction." A glance outside told him those goons were already being taken into custody. Hopefully they would be able to match their DNA to whatever had been recovered from Martin's battered body.

"Since I'm going to go to jail anyway..." She lifted the gun she must have been holding beneath the table and pointed the barrel at him.

He was so surprised that he just laughed. He had survived terrorists and mobsters and was about to be taken out by an old, gray-haired lady with a gun?

CLAIRE NEVER SAW Special Agent Ash Stryker again. Ash was fine, though; he had brought Martin's killer to justice weeks ago. But Claire hadn't heard that announcement from his lips; she had learned that good news from his friends Blaine and Maggie Campbell.

She wanted what they had. The young couple's love and happiness reminded her of her father and Pam's. And seeing them together had reminded her that she wanted that kind of loving relationship for herself. She wouldn't find that with Ash. He wouldn't open himself up to his friends; he wouldn't open himself up to anyone.

She loved him, but she could love again. Maybe…

Maybe there was someone else out there for her. Someone who would actually return her love. That thought—that hope—had compelled her to try another speed dating event.

Unfortunately it was at the Waterview Inn, the same hotel with the same grapevine carpeting in the dining room where she had met Special Agent Ash Stryker. He had no reason to be there now. He no longer thought she was a traitor to her country. So he didn't have to stop her from selling out national security.

Apparently he didn't have to see her ever again.

The bell dinged, drawing Claire's attention back to the man sitting across from her. His blond hair was thinning and his waistline thickening. But he probably wasn't that much older than she was. Nor was there any mark on his finger from ever wearing a ring. Still he hadn't interested or attracted her—not like Ash had.

The blond man had been talking, but she hadn't heard a word he had uttered the entire five minutes. He hadn't seemed to mind that she hadn't participated in that conversation, though.

He grinned and heartily shook her hand like a politician confident that he had her vote. She wasn't even sure that she'd told him her name. But apparently he didn't care that he knew nothing about her.

Ash knew about her. He knew more about her than anyone else ever had. He knew about her past and what she wanted for her future.

Maybe that was why he hadn't come to see her again after he had arrested Martin's killer. Maybe he'd known that there was no point in seeing her again when he couldn't give her what she wanted. A relationship. A family.

The bell dinged again, signaling the beginning of the next five minutes. Claire barely glanced up to greet her new potential match. So she caught just a glimpse of black hair, blue eyes and chiseled features as he settled onto the chair across from her. He reached his hand across the table and introduced himself, "Hello, my name is Ash Stryker."

She stared at his hand and remembered how it had caressed her body, how it had made her skin tingle. She didn't reach for it. She couldn't touch him again and not want him. Already she ached for him. Or maybe she had never stopped.

"So what's your name?" he asked as if he really had no idea.

She glared at him but said nothing, refusing to participate in whatever game he was playing with her.

"We only have five minutes," he reminded her. "Aren't you going to speak to me?"

"Why?" she asked. "What cover are you going under now?"

Amusement twinkled in his bright blue eyes. "Isn't it kind of presumptuous to discuss going under covers? We've only just met."

She sighed. "No, we haven't."

But she wished that they had. Then she could just enjoy how handsome he was with that thick black hair and those bright blue eyes. She could enjoy how funny he could be, even though he wasn't amusing her much now. And if they had really just met, she wouldn't know yet that they had nothing in common, that they would have no future.

"No, we haven't just met," he admitted. "In fact, it feels like we've known each other forever. Like there wasn't a time that you weren't a part of my life, that you weren't a part of me…"

Surprise had her gasping. She hadn't realized that he felt that way, too—as if they were parts of a whole. That was why she'd felt so empty and incomplete without him.

He reached for something.

She tensed and nervously glanced around the dining room because usually when he reached for something, it was his weapon. But he didn't pull a gun. Instead, he placed a gift bag on the table between them.

"What's this?" she asked. Just as she hadn't reached for his hand, she didn't reach for it, either. She just stared at the glittery red gift bag.

"Look inside," he urged her, and now his eyes brightened with excitement. And in that moment he reminded her of her father, who had barely been able to wait until her birthday or Christmas to give her presents. He hadn't been able to wait to see her reaction to the gift he'd chosen for her that he'd been pretty certain she would love.

Why did Ash think she would love this gift?

Her hands trembling slightly, she reached inside the bag. Her fingertips skimmed over cool glass, and she pulled out a musical snow globe. The music automatically began to play. It was the song to which they had danced last at the piano bar. *I could have danced all night...*

She really could have and wished that they had. Inside the snow globe a dark-haired man spun a blonde woman around a dance floor. Claire shook the globe and sparkling confetti rained down around them.

She couldn't stop staring at it in awe. "Where did you find this?"

"I asked your dad who made that one for him that you love so much," he replied. "Thankfully they were still in business and willing to make this one for me."

He drew her attention from the globe to him, and she asked in shock, "You talked to my dad?"

"Yes, of course," he said in that matter-of-fact tone that had once infuriated her. "I had to ask his permission."

"Permission for what?" she asked, completely befuddled why he would talk to her father. "To make me a globe?"

"I asked for his permission to propose to you." He dropped to his knee on his side of the table. "Will you marry me, Claire Molenski?"

Was she dreaming? She must have fallen asleep while the last man had been talking, and she had dreamed up this perfect fantasy.

The bell dinged.

"Claire, you have to answer me," Ash said. "We're out of time."

Panic attacked her just as it had the last time she'd

met Special Agent Ash Stryker at a speed dating event. She couldn't believe what he was saying, what he was doing. She couldn't believe that any of it was real or really happening. That panic overwhelmed her, making it hard for her to think or even breathe. She needed air. Now. Instead of answering him, she stood up so quickly that she knocked over her chair. Then she grabbed her purse and ran from the room.

"You DID IT AGAIN," a bald-headed man said from beside Ash. "You scared her off." He must have been at that other event.

Ash would like to believe that he wasn't the one who had scared her off that night. But tonight he definitely was to blame. He'd thought she would love the globe... because he had thought she might love him.

He couldn't believe how wrong he'd been. He shouldn't have listened to Blaine and what he'd said about her hobbling up on a sprained ankle to check on him. That hadn't been out of love but out of concern for a fellow human being.

Ash was definitely not the man she wanted. But he'd thought he might be able to convince her that he could be that man. He could give her what she wanted. He had been so wrong...

He picked up the globe and stared at that dancing couple. They looked so happy, so in love as they twirled deliriously around that dance floor. The dark-haired man in a suit, the blonde woman in a red dress.

Ash had wanted to give her that perfect memory like when she'd skated with her father. But maybe he had only reminded her of the nightmare, that they had nearly been killed in an alley behind that piano bar. Maybe he had reminded her that his life was dangerous and since they'd met, he'd brought that danger into her life. He didn't blame her for running from him.

He sighed and shoved the globe back in the gift bag. Then he headed from the room. Maybe he should have run right out of the room after her. Maybe he should have tried to catch her. But even though his leg had healed enough to run, his pride was stung too much to chase her. His heart was hurting. He felt more than disappointment. He felt devastation.

He had been so hopeful that she would at least consider his proposal. He hadn't expected an immediate yes. He'd realized that she would have to think about it, that he might have to convince her.

Hair lifted on his nape as an eerie sense of foreboding overwhelmed him. Somebody was watching him. He stopped and glanced around the dimly lit lobby.

"You talked to my father?" she asked, her soft voice reaching him from the shadows. She stood just outside the doors to the dining room.

"Yes," he replied. Her father had been everything Ash had thought he would be considering he had earned so much love and loyalty from his daughter. Mr. Molenski had been warm and welcoming and even understanding when Ash had explained what a fool he'd been to try to resist his feelings for Claire. "I guess it was presumptuous of me."

"What was presumptuous of you?"

"Meeting him." A man shouldn't talk to a father until he was certain that the daughter returned his feelings. "I met Pam, too. She's very nice." She had been every bit as warm and welcoming as her new husband had been.

"Are they having fun?" Claire anxiously asked. She loved so deeply—her family, her friends, even her work...

Why couldn't she have loved him?

"They seem very happy," Ash assured her. "He was worried about you, though." Until Mr. Molenski had met Ash and gotten his promise that he would make his daughter happy. Too bad he had already broken that promise.

She sighed and stepped from the shadows to join him in the middle of the lobby. "I talked to him a few days ago. I wish I hadn't called him. I knew he would hear it in my voice and worry."

"Hear what?" he asked. "You didn't talk to him until after everyone had been caught and you were safe again. What did he hear?"

"Me," she said with a heavy sigh. "Missing you…"

Maybe he had reason to hope; it burgeoned in his chest again. Maybe he hadn't read her completely wrong. "You missed me?"

She gave a brief, reluctant nod.

"I hoped you would," he admitted.

She glared at him slightly resentfully. "Is that why you stayed away?"

"I wanted to talk to your dad before I saw you again," he said. The minute he saw her again, he knew he would propose, so he had wanted her father's permission first.

"But the protection detail had been pulled off him and Pam," she said, "so you must have hacked into my itinerary for him to find out where he would be now."

He offered her a sheepish smile. "I have some skills, too," he murmured.

"You're a hacker," she teased him. "I could have you arrested for breaking into my personal files."

"You probably could," he agreed. "I also stayed away because it took some time to have that globe made." He had wanted every detail to be perfect.

She reached out for the bag and lifted the globe from it. Tears glistened in her eyes as she studied it.

"It was worth every minute spent waiting for it," she said. "It's so beautiful."

"You're so beautiful…" She was wearing the red dress again; he loved that damn dress. But he loved what was in it even more. "And so smart and funny and sexy…" He couldn't imagine his life without her in it now. The past few weeks had been hell without her—far worse than any deployment or undercover assignment.

She glanced from the globe to him and back. "Did you really just propose in there?"

A grin teased his lips at how disbelieving she was. But then she had overheard that ridiculous claim he'd made to Blaine. He nodded. "Yes, I really asked you to be my wife."

"It's not part of some cover?" she asked. "You're not going to pose as my fiancé because I'm in danger again?"

"I don't want to be your fiancé as a cover," he said. "I want to be your fiancé for real. I want to be your husband for life."

Hope replaced the disbelief on her face, and her lips curved into a slight smile. She nodded.

He grinned as happiness overwhelmed him. It seemed like she was saying yes. "There's something else inside the bag. You must have missed it."

She reached into it again and pulled out a red velvet box. Her hand trembled as she held it. Her voice low with awe, she murmured, "You really are proposing…"

"Yes," he replied.

She popped open the box and stared down at the brilliant round diamond.

"Are *you* saying yes?" he asked hopefully.

"I didn't think it was real," she said.

"This isn't part of an undercover assignment," he assured her. "This is real. My feelings for you are real." And no matter how much time passed, they would never go away.

"I thought you coming here with this globe and that proposal was a dream," she said. "I thought that you didn't need anybody and never would."

He groaned at what a fool he had been to ever think that. "I was wrong."

"Is this wrong?" she asked as she held up the ring. "Do we have anything in common?"

He tapped the glass of the globe, and the music began to play again. "We love to dance."

She nodded.

"We love to kiss."

She smiled.

"I love you," he said. "I didn't know how much I could love someone until I fell in love with you. And yet I love you more every day. With every smile you smile, every word you speak, I love you more."

Her breath caught and tears welled in her eyes. He didn't know if those were tears of happiness or regret that she didn't return his feelings.

Then she said it back. "And I love you. I love how heroic you are, how strong and yet graceful and funny, too. I love you so much."

His heart pounded hard with excitement and happiness. She loved him. "I would say that we have more in common than most people do."

"I'm a slob," she reminded him.

"I love that about you, too," he responded. "And we'll hire a cleaning lady."

She laughed and then she was in his arms, hers winding around his neck and she rose up on tiptoe and pressed her lips to his. "I love everything about you."

He kissed her back but lifted his mouth long enough to ask, "I'm not too uptight? Too much of a suit?"

"I love that about you, too," she said, and her green eyes sparkled with that love she professed. "You're perfect..."

"I am perfect," he readily agreed, "but only for you. I will give you all the love and attention I can."

Her smile dimmed for a moment. "I'll be happy with whatever you can give. I understand how busy you are, keeping the world safe and all."

He grinned at her exaggeration. "You keep the world safe, too."

"You know that I didn't really quit?" she asked. "That I'm still working for the company."

Nowak had only put out the press release to protect her. And it had worked. "I know everything about you."

"I do intend to work less, though," she said as if warning him. "And pretty much only from home, like Leslie does."

"I'm cutting back, too," he said. "I'm going to do more administrative work—concentrate on training and leading more agents to save the world."

She gasped in shock. "What? Why?"

"I don't want to go undercover anymore," he said. "Not unless I'm going undercover with you."

Her smile returned, brighter than before, and she picked something out of her bottomless bag. A key card for a room. She waved it in his face. "Want to go under covers with me now?"

He shook his head. "Not until you give me an answer, Claire. Will you marry me?"

"Yes, I will," she replied ecstatically. "I will marry you!"

He swept her up in his arms and carried her toward the elevators. He couldn't wait for the honeymoon. He had to have her now and every night for the rest of their lives.

* * * * *

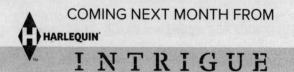

COMING NEXT MONTH FROM

HARLEQUIN

INTRIGUE

Available April 21, 2015

#1563 SHOWDOWN AT SHADOW JUNCTION
Big "D" Dads: The Daltons • by Joanna Wayne
When Jade Dalton escapes a ruthless kidnapper on the trail of a
multimillion-dollar necklace, Navy SEAL Booker Knox will do whatever
it takes to protect the beautiful event planner. Failure isn't an option.

#1564 TWO SOULS HOLLOW
The Gates • by Paula Graves
Ginny Coltrane might hold the key to proving Anson Daughtry's
innocence. But when Ginny is dragged into a drug war, Anson may be
her only hope of escaping with her life.

#1565 SCENE OF THE CRIME: KILLER COVE
by Carla Cassidy
Accused of murder, Bo McBride has finally returned to Lost Lagoon to
clear his name—with the help of sexy Claire Silver. But as they investigate,
it doesn't take long to realize that danger stalks Claire...

#1566 NAVY SEAL JUSTICE
Covert Cowboys, Inc. • by Elle James
After former Navy SEAL James Monahan and FBI agent Melissa Bradley's
mutual friend goes missing, they join forces to find him. But as a band of
dangerous criminals closes in, survival means trusting each other—their
toughest mission yet.

#1567 COWBOY INCOGNITO
The Brothers of Hastings Ridge Ranch • by Alice Sharpe
A roadtrip to uncover Zane Doe's identity exposes his *real* connection to
Kinsey Frost—and the murderous intentions of those once close to her. Now
Zane must protect her from someone who wants to silence her for good.

#1568 UNDER SUSPICION
Bayou Bonne Chance • by Mallory Kane
Undercover NSA agent Zach Winters vows to solve his best friend's
murder. With the criminals closing in, Zach will risk his own life to protect
a vulnerable widow and her beautiful bodyguard, Madeleine Tierney—the
woman he can't imagine saying goodbye to.

REQUEST YOUR FREE BOOKS!
2 FREE NOVELS PLUS 2 FREE GIFTS!

H HARLEQUIN®

INTRIGUE®

BREATHTAKING ROMANTIC SUSPENSE

YES! Please send me 2 FREE Harlequin Intrigue® novels and my 2 FREE gifts (gifts are worth about $10). After receiving them, if I don't wish to receive any more books, I can return the shipping statement marked "cancel." If I don't cancel, I will receive 6 brand-new novels every month and be billed just $4.74 per book in the U.S. or $5.24 per book in Canada. That's a savings of at least 14% off the cover price! It's quite a bargain! Shipping and handling is just 50¢ per book in the U.S. and 75¢ per book in Canada.* I understand that accepting the 2 free books and gifts places me under no obligation to buy anything. I can always return a shipment and cancel at any time. Even if I never buy another book, the two free books and gifts are mine to keep forever.

182/382 HDN F42N

Name	(PLEASE PRINT)

Address	Apt. #

City	State/Prov.	Zip/Postal Code

Signature (if under 18, a parent or guardian must sign)

Mail to the **Harlequin® Reader Service:**
IN U.S.A.: P.O. Box 1867, Buffalo, NY 14240-1867
IN CANADA: P.O. Box 609, Fort Erie, Ontario L2A 5X3
**Are you a subscriber to Harlequin Intrigue books
and want to receive the larger-print edition?
Call 1-800-873-8635 or visit www.ReaderService.com.**

* Terms and prices subject to change without notice. Prices do not include applicable taxes. Sales tax applicable in N.Y. Canadian residents will be charged applicable taxes. Offer not valid in Quebec. This offer is limited to one order per household. Not valid for current subscribers to Harlequin Intrigue books. All orders subject to credit approval. Credit or debit balances in a customer's account(s) may be offset by any other outstanding balance owed by or to the customer. Please allow 4 to 6 weeks for delivery. Offer available while quantities last.

Your Privacy—The Harlequin® Reader Service is committed to protecting your privacy. Our Privacy Policy is available online at www.ReaderService.com or upon request from the Harlequin Reader Service.

We make a portion of our mailing list available to reputable third parties that offer products we believe may interest you. If you prefer that we not exchange your name with third parties, or if you wish to clarify or modify your communication preferences, please visit us at www.ReaderService.com/consumerchoice or write to us at Harlequin Reader Service Preference Service, P.O. Box 9062, Buffalo, NY 14269. Include your complete name and address.

HI13R

SPECIAL EXCERPT FROM

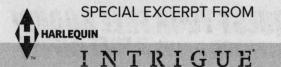

HARLEQUIN

INTRIGUE

Bo McBride, accused but never arrested for the murder of his girlfriend two years ago, has finally returned to Lost Lagoon, Mississippi, to clear his name with Claire Silber's help. But it doesn't take long for them to realize that real danger stalks Claire.

Read on for a sneak preview of
SCENE OF THE CRIME: KILLER COVE,
the latest crime scene book from
New York Times *bestselling author*
Carla Cassidy.

"So, your turn. Tell me what you've been doing for the last two years," Claire asked. "Have you made yourself a new, happy life? Found a new love? I heard through the grapevine that you're living in Jackson now."

Bo nodded at the same time the sound of rain splattered against the window. "I opened a little bar and grill, Bo's Place, although it's nothing like the original." His dark brows tugged together in a frown, as if remembering the highly successful business he'd had here in town before he was ostracized.

He took another big drink and then continued, "There's no new woman in my life. I don't even have friends. Hell, I'm not even sure what I'm doing here with you."

"You're here because I'm a bossy woman," she replied. She got up to refill his glass. "And I thought you could use an extra friend while you're here."

She handed him the fresh drink and then curled back up

in the corner of the sofa. The rain fell steadily now. She turned on the end table lamp as the room darkened with the storm.

For a few minutes they remained silent. She could tell by his distant stare toward the opposite wall that he was lost inside his head.

Despite his somber expression, she couldn't help but feel a physical attraction to him that she'd never felt before. Still, that wasn't what had driven her to seek contact with him, to invite him into her home. She had an ulterior motive.

A low rumble of thunder seemed to pull him out of his head. He focused on her and offered a small smile of apology. "Sorry about that. I got lost in thoughts of everything I need to get done before I leave town."

"I wanted to talk to you about that," she said.

He raised a dark brow. "About all the things I need to take care of?"

"No, about you leaving town."

"What about it?"

She drew a deep breath, knowing she was putting her nose in business that wasn't her own, and yet unable to stop herself. "Doesn't it bother you knowing that Shelly's murderer is still walking these streets, free as a bird?"

His eyes narrowed slightly. "Why are you so sure I'm innocent?" he asked.

Don't miss
SCENE OF THE CRIME: KILLER COVE
by New York Times *bestselling author Carla Cassidy,*
available May 2015 wherever
Harlequin® Intrigue books and ebooks are sold.

www.Harlequin.com

THE WORLD IS BETTER WITH

Romance

214

Harlequin has everything from contemporary, passionate and heartwarming to suspenseful and inspirational stories.

Whatever your mood, we have a romance just for you!